P9-APH-467

"Luke," she said simply, her voice, a bit more mature, but still as soft and melodious as he remembered.

"It's Dr. Wynter now."

He regretted his response the moment it left his mouth. It probably sounded as though he was flaunting the medical degree he'd fought long and hard to earn. Instead he'd only meant to validate himself in her eyes. To let her know a lot had changed since her brother had died and she'd shut him out of her life.

She could trust him now. He was older, wiser. He wasn't the teenager she'd once loved.

Yet her gaze still had the power to take his breath away.

Dear Reader,

After writing four books in the Bayside Bachelors series, I received many letters and emails from readers, asking me to create Dr. Luke Wynter's story. So here it is!

I hope you enjoy reading *Daddy on Call* as much as I did writing it. As some of you may have guessed, I'm a firm believer in second chances and new beginnings. And this story has it all.

During the month of April, I'll be hosting a special contest on my Web site at www.JudyDuarte.com. The winner will receive a six-month subscription to the Special Edition book club and have a choice of five autographed books from my backlist. There will be prizes for the runners up, too. (Winners will be announced on or around May 15, 2007.)

If you'd like to enter, all you have to do is provide the name of the flower that represents the theme in this book. You'll find the answer within the pages, but just in case you'd like a hint, I'll leave you with the words of Mark Twain:

Forgiveness is the fragrance the violet sheds on the heel that crushed it.

Happy reading,

Judy

DADDY ON CALL

JUDY DUARTE

SPECIAL EDITION®

Published by Silhouette Books

America's Publisher of Contemporary Romance

If you purchased this book without a cover you should be aware
that this book is stolen property. It was reported as "unsold and
destroyed" to the publisher, and neither the author nor the
publisher has received any payment for this "stripped book."

SILHOUETTE BOOKS

®

ISBN-13: 978-0-373-24822-3
ISBN-10: 0-373-24822-9

DADDY ON CALL

Copyright © 2007 by Judy Duarte

All rights reserved. Except for use in any review, the reproduction
or utilization of this work in whole or in part in any form by any
electronic, mechanical or other means, now known or hereafter
invented, including xerography, photocopying and recording, or in
any information storage or retrieval system, is forbidden without
the written permission of the editorial office, Silhouette Books,
233 Broadway, New York, NY 10279 U.S.A.

This is a work of fiction. Names, characters, places and incidents are
either the product of the author's imagination or are used fictitiously, and
any resemblance to actual persons, living or dead, business establishments,
events or locales is entirely coincidental.

This edition published by arrangement with Harlequin Books S.A.

® and TM are trademarks of Harlequin Books S.A., used under license.
Trademarks indicated with ® are registered in the United States Patent
and Trademark Office, the Canadian Trade Marks Office and in other
countries.

Visit Silhouette Books at www.eHarlequin.com

Printed in U.S.A.

Books by Judy Duarte

Silhouette Special Edition

Cowboy Courage #1458
Family Practice #1511
Almost Perfect #1540
Big Sky Baby #1563
The Virgin's Makeover #1593
Bluegrass Baby #1598
The Rich Man's Son #1634
*Hailey's Hero #1659
*Their Secret Son #1667
Their Unexpected Family #1676
*Worth Fighting For #1684
*The Matchmakers' Daddy #1689
His Mother's Wedding #1731
Call Me Cowboy #1743
The Perfect Wife #1773
Rock-A-Bye Rancher #1784
Daddy on Call #1822

Silhouette Books

Double Destiny
   "Second Chance"

*Bayside Bachelors

JUDY DUARTE

always knew there was a book inside her, but since English was her least favorite subject in school, she never considered herself a writer. An avid reader who enjoys a happy ending, Judy couldn't shake the dream of creating a book of her own.

Her dream became a reality in March of 2002, when the Silhouette Special Edition line released Judy's first book, *Cowboy Courage*. Since then, she has sold nineteen more novels. In July of 2005, Judy won the prestigious Reader's Choice Award for *The Rich Man's Son*.

Judy makes her home near the beach in Southern California. When she's not cooped up in her writing cave, she's spending time with her somewhat enormous, but delightfully close family.

You can write to Judy c/o Silhouette Books, 233 Broadway, Suite 1001, New York, NY 10237. You can also contact her at JudyDuarte@aol.com or through her Web site, www.JudyDuarte.com.

To Colleen Holth, Laura Astleford, Gail Duarte,
Lydia Bustos and Gloria Duarte.
I grew up with brothers; my sisters came later.

Chapter One

Dr. Luke Wynter had only started his shift an hour ago, but he'd already sent his third broken bone of the day up to radiology, stitched up a nasty wound on an elderly woman's brow, admitted a five-year-old for dehydration and diagnosed three cases of the flu that had been plaguing the area.

"Doctor, we've got an ambulance coming in with a pregnant woman who's been badly beaten by her boyfriend."

Luke glanced up from the chart he'd been reading and addressed Marge Bagley, a fifty-something RN who could run circles around the first-year residents and mentor those who'd acquired their fair share of rotations. "What's the estimated time of arrival?"

"Three minutes or less."

He nodded, then quickly completed his task.

Marge was one of Luke's favorite nurses. Together, she and he worked the night shift at Oceana General. He wouldn't say they'd become friends, since they never associated outside the hospital, but they'd developed a healthy respect for one another and had shared plenty of overbrewed coffee.

Luke had a few friends, mostly the guys who'd become known as Logan's Heroes, a group of men who'd once been delinquents but had turned their lives around thanks to the guidance of Detective Harry Logan. But for the most part, he didn't socialize much. Hell, how could he when he worked nights and required a few z's to function?

"Showtime," Marge whispered, as she nodded toward the paramedics rushing through the door.

"Take her into room three," Luke said as he walked alongside the stretcher, conducting a quick assessment of the victim's injuries and taking note of the vitals being announced by Craig Elwood, one of the paramedics.

"Who did this to her?" Luke asked.

"Apparently, a jealous boyfriend. He held the cops at bay for a while, then slipped out the back."

The bastard had done a real number on her, and Luke hoped the police caught the guy. He'd be facing assault charges if she lived, homicide if she didn't.

Marge, who walked with them, asked, "Does she have any family members coming in?"

Luke knew the RN was asking about next of kin.

"She's got a friend coming in behind us, driving her own vehicle. Her name's Lonnie, I think. The patient's name is Carrie Summers."

Luke nodded, then ordered a battery of tests and scans. The patient—or rather *the victim* in this case—had suffered a dislocated jaw, a head injury and possible internal bleeding. Luke wasn't sure whether he could save her life, let alone that of the baby she carried.

But he was up for a fight. In fact, he always had been, only now he battled death.

"Who's the resident neurosurgeon?" Luke asked Marge.

"Dick Wofford. And I've already called him. I also paged Arlene Gray. She's on duty in obstetrics tonight."

Luke liked working with Marge. She seemed to know what he was thinking. During the downtime, when they were free to make light of things, he called her "Radar," like the character on *M.A.S.H.*

Always one to dish it back, Marge referred to him as Hot Lips, although he suspected it had nothing to do with the classic television show and everything to do with a particular blonde lab technician who'd kissed and told.

As Luke worked on the patient and ordered more tests and scans, Dick Wofford arrived, followed by Arlene Gray. Together, they decided the best treatment for mother and child. Neither specialist was any more optimistic than Luke, and both commended him for his treatment thus far.

Marge, who'd slipped out of the room momentarily, returned. "The victim's friend just arrived, and I sent her to the waiting room near the ICU."

It was, Luke realized, the best place for the friend to wait. The neurosurgeon would be making the call on whether the critically injured woman needed surgery or not, but either way, she would be spending time in intensive care.

After passing the patient on to the specialists, Luke headed for the waiting room to find Carrie's friend.

Talking to loved ones was his least favorite part of the job. His bedside manner had never won him any accolades, but he didn't care. He couldn't afford to let the patients or their families get to him. Keeping some emotional distance allowed him to do what he did best—save lives.

He paused in the doorway and scanned the handful of people waiting for word on friends and family members. An elderly couple rested on a sofa near the television, holding hands. A middle-aged man sat alone in the corner, reading a magazine, while a dark-haired woman wearing a silver clip in her hair stood at the window, looking into the dark of night.

"Who's here with Carrie Summers?" he asked.

The woman peering out the window turned to face him. When her gaze met his, the past slammed into him, causing his mind to numb and his pulse to jam.

Recognition crossed her face. Shock, too.

He supposed he couldn't blame her, since she'd pretty much considered him a juvenile delinquent

the last time he'd seen her. And here he was now—
the attending physician in the E.R. of one of the
county's busiest hospitals.

Of course, the fact that he'd turned his life
around and had morphed into a doctor had surprised a lot of people.

She neither smiled nor frowned, which made it
tough to regroup, to gather his wits. Or to rein in
emotions that threatened to run amok.

Leilani Stephens had been his first love, and not
many days went by that he didn't think about her.
Dream about her.

As a kid, he'd been in awe of her lovely hula-girl
shape, year-round tropical tan and knockout smile.
But it had been more than her physical attributes that
had caught his eye and kicked up his hormones. Her
innocence and sweet nature had slapped him with a
full-blown case of puppy love.

Even so, it hadn't been her memory that had
haunted him for the past twelve years. It had been her
parting words, the anger in her voice and the tears in
her eyes that had burned into his soul.

She'd held Luke responsible for her younger
brother's death. And she'd never forgiven him for it.

When push came to shove, he supposed he'd never
forgiven himself, either. No matter how much time
had passed. Or how big a change he'd made in his life.

But he wasn't the only one who'd changed.
Leilani was no longer the teenager he'd once loved,
either. No longer the seventeen-year-old Polynesian

beauty with silky, waist-length black hair who could turn a guy's heart inside out. She'd grown older and undoubtedly wiser.

Yet her gaze still had the power to take his breath away.

"Luke," she said simply, her voice a bit more mature, but still as soft and melodious as he remembered.

"It's Dr. Wynter now."

He regretted his response the moment it left his mouth. It probably sounded as though he was flaunting the medical degree he'd fought long and hard to earn. Instead he'd only meant to validate himself in her eyes. To let her know a lot had changed since her brother had died and she'd shut him out of her life.

That she could trust him now.

She cleared her throat as though still trying to take it all in and decide how she felt about it. "The nurse mentioned Carrie was being examined by Dr. Wynter. But I had no idea…"

"I can understand why."

"How is she?"

"Stable," he said. "For now. But she's critical. Come with me. Let's talk in private."

He led her down the hall to the room set aside for giving a patient's family bad news. Not that he would paint a dark picture. It was too early to tell for sure. But the guy who beat Carrie had nearly killed her, and she was a long way from being out of the woods.

It was a painful walk—more so than any other

he'd had to make. His mind scurried to find the right words. But not so much about her friend.

All that had separated them before jumped to the forefront, just as real and heartbreaking as the day she left San Diego and never came back.

As they entered the small room, with its pale green walls and living room-style atmosphere, he asked Leilani to have a seat.

She chose the floral-print sofa, but sat on the edge as if wanting to bolt.

He could relate. He felt like hightailing it out of there, too.

For some reason, he would have preferred to be outdoors when he talked to her, away from the four walls that sometimes closed in on him when he was faced with grieving friends and family members who struggled with the shock of an accident, illness or death.

He might be a whiz when it came to treating bullet holes, knife wounds and broken bones, but he wasn't good at handing out sympathy along with the tissues or saying the right thing. Hell, if he'd had any gifts in the emotional support department, maybe his mom wouldn't have chosen to end it all a few years back.

Luke took a seat on a beige vinyl recliner. To say neither of them had expected to see the other, to be sitting across the table face-to-face, was an understatement of gigantic proportions.

"Leilani," he said, realizing that her name, as Hawaiian as the island on which she'd grown up, slipped off his tongue as though the last twelve years hadn't gone by. As though they were still kids tripping over their hormones.

Yet the past hovered over them like a vulture ready to swoop down and consume the remnants of innocence—her brother's and hers. As much as he'd wanted to apologize years ago—to explain his version of the story—that wasn't why she was sitting across from him. Nor was it what she wanted to hear right now.

Luke always remained detached from his patients—for their sake as well as his own. He merely assessed injuries and illnesses, then provided emergency treatment until the patients could be passed to the appropriate specialists or sent home to recover. He struggled to do the same this evening, but it wasn't working very well.

He suspected it was because he'd let Leilani down before and was hoping to provide her with a better outcome this time.

"Is Carrie going to die?" Those pretty golden-brown eyes searched his for answers he didn't have.

"It's too early to know. I won't beat around the bush. She's hurt badly. And her pregnancy complicates things."

"How's the baby?"

"Alive. I'm afraid we don't know much right now. But the neurosurgeon and obstetrician will determine the best treatment for her."

Her gaze, wide-eyed and luminous, lanced his chest, making him feel like an awkward adolescent with a crush on the new girl at school—an exotic beauty who'd been blessed with the best genetics her Anglo father and Hawaiian mother could offer.

And in spite of the voice inside begging him to step back, to pass not only the patient on to other doctors, but to pass Leilani on, too, he found it tough to do so.

"How are you holding up?" he asked.

"Me?"

Leilani wasn't sure what to tell him. Needless to say, she was deeply concerned about her friend and the baby. But running into Luke Wynter had never crossed her mind. And the fact that he'd turned his life around merely added more surprise to the mix.

"I'm okay," she said, although that wasn't entirely true. There was a lot of history between the two of them, and Luke didn't know the half of it.

A wave of guilt rolled over her, as well as the ever-present resentment she felt whenever she'd thought of him over the past twelve years.

"I didn't realize you were back in town," he said. "I'd heard you relocated to Los Angeles."

"I'm just visiting my aunt." She glanced at the garnet ring on her right hand, an heirloom that once belonged to her mother, and fingered it. When she looked up, she added, "And I also came to see Carrie. She's a friend I met in Los Angeles. She relocated a while back...."

He nodded as though that made sense and didn't press for more information. She was glad; she wasn't ready to renew their friendship.

Their *friendship?*

God. They'd become involved as teenagers on the cusp of adulthood.

Young lovers who'd been wrong for each other.

A nurse poked her head through the doorway. "Excuse me, Dr. Wynter. But there's an important call for you from Dr. Kim. And those lab results for Mrs. Rosenberg are back. You told me to let you know the minute they were in."

Luke nodded.

He'd grown up and filled out, Leilani realized, yet he still wore his hair the same—attractively unkempt. And apparently he didn't shave every day, which left him with the rugged look that had always appealed to her.

"If you'll excuse me," he said, his voice settling over her like a sense of déjà vu.

"Of course."

She was pleased to know Luke had made something of himself—something noble and respectful. Yet the fact that he had also made her feel guilty about the secret she'd kept.

A secret she'd decided to keep when Luke had been little more than a delinquent and she'd expected him to spend the bulk of his life behind bars—especially after her brother's death.

When she left San Diego, she'd had every intention of forgetting Luke Wynter, but she hadn't been able to.

Not when their eleven-year-old son reminded her of him daily.

* * *

Early the next morning, when his shift was over, Luke did something he rarely did; he went to check on a patient he'd handed over to specialists.

But it wasn't just any patient.

It was Carrie Summers, who was in a coma.

He read her chart, then spoke to the nurse who'd been assigned to her. Carrie was, so far, holding her own.

On his way out of the ICU, he stopped by the waiting room where he spotted Leilani seated on a sofa. She was wearing the same white blouse and black slacks she'd had on last night, rumpled clothing that indicated she hadn't gone home to sleep.

Somewhere along the way she'd unclipped the silver barrette she'd been wearing and let her hair down. It was shoulder length now, but just as glossy as it had been before. Just as tempting to touch.

She glanced up when he entered. "Is something wrong?"

Yeah, there was something wrong. He'd been getting by just fine until she snuck back into his life. And now she had him dancing around the past like a Mexican jumping bean. "No problem. So far, so good."

She merely stared at him, as though wondering why he'd stopped by. And he was just as perplexed as she was. After all, twelve years ago she'd made no secret of the fact that she no longer considered him a friend, let alone a lover. And he'd never been one to plead or beg.

But there was something drawing him to her. Something that was unsettled, unfinished. Unsaid.

So he made an excuse for stopping by. "I just got off duty and wanted to check on her before heading home."

That reason ought to fly, especially since Leilani had no way of knowing that wasn't his usual style.

"You work nights?" she asked.

"Yeah."

"Must be tough."

Not for Luke. "I like the action. More gunshots, stabbings."

"I suppose you'd find that exciting."

He wasn't sure what she meant. He hoped she wasn't referring to his early years, when he'd gotten into his share of scuffles. Or that month he'd spent at juvenile hall. Actually, he was talking about having the opportunity to practice emergency medicine, to use the skills he'd perfected.

"I never expected you to become a doctor," she added.

Neither had Luke. It had taken tragedy, heartbreak and a lucky draw like crossing paths with Harry Logan for him to make that kind of a turn. But he supposed she wouldn't care to hear about it. "I've always had an aptitude for science."

"I know. You tutored me in chemistry, remember?"

He remembered everything. The scent of her as

she leaned over him in the library, the way her hair sluiced over his cheek. The difficulty he had focusing on the problem at hand, rather than his raging hormones. "Thanks to me, you got an *A*."

"No. I believe it was a *B*-plus. But it would have been an *F* without your help."

God, it was strange, skating around the past. But he wasn't ready to jump head-first into it, either. So he decided to use a little humor to take the edge off the reality. "I had to knock several honor students on their butts in order to have a chance to tutor the pretty new girl."

Actually, there was a lot of truth to that. The moment he'd laid eyes on her, he'd been swept off his feet and would have done anything just to be alone with her.

He wanted to ask if she'd ever gone on to college, like she'd planned. Whether she'd gotten a degree of any kind. But that would only lead them to the reason she'd left town.

And the reason she'd never talked to him again.

Instead, he nodded toward the sofa. "I see you spent the night here."

"Carrie doesn't have any family, so I felt as though I ought to stay." Leilani combed her hand through her hair, her fingers snagging on a tangle before busting free. "And I agreed to be her baby's godmother and promised to look after him if…anything happened to her."

"Dr. Gray has managed to stave off contractions,"

he said, figuring Arlene had already told her the baby's chances of survival if it was born now.

"I know." She bit down on her bottom lip, something she used to do when they were friends.

And lovers.

At the time, Leilani's heart was as big as the Pacific, although little good that did him. Once her brother died, she'd refused to hear Luke's side of the story, refused to let him apologize. Would she now? Had enough time passed?

Had anything changed?

Not on the part of his hormones. He couldn't help being drawn to her.

It was amazing. Even after all she'd been through and then dozing all night in a chair on top of that, she looked damn good. Prettier than ever, he decided. And just as out of reach.

He wasn't crazy enough to think that they could ever be lovers again, but he wanted her to know how sorry he was about her brother's death, about his part in it.

"Leilani," he said, hoping to get her away from a hospital setting. "Would it be all right if I bought you a cup of coffee?"

She didn't respond right away, and he wasn't sure what to expect when she did.

Was it too much to hope that she might find it in her heart to forgive him?

If so, he might be able to forgive himself.

Chapter Two

How about a cup of coffee?

Leilani opened her mouth to decline, but at the same time she was eager to learn more about Carrie, to hear the E.R. doctor's opinion.

"In fact," Luke added, "you could probably use some breakfast."

She was torn. She hated to leave her friend's side, yet was desperate for Luke's prognosis for both mother and child. "All right. But I'm afraid I look a mess."

"No, you don't. You look like a concerned friend." He stepped aside, allowing her to exit first, then escorted her down the hall and to the elevator.

It felt weird walking with him again and was reminiscent of the times they'd strode the halls when they were seniors in high school. As much as she dreaded being alone with a man she'd loved once upon a time, she struggled with the same attraction, the same excitement his rebellious smile provoked.

The fact that they had a son together only heightened her discomfort.

Her heels clicked on the linoleum as they strode through the corridor, and inadvertently, her shoulder brushed against his, warming her from the inside out. Funny how, after all this time, his touch could still do that to her.

The various medical personnel they passed along the way—lab techs, nurses' aides, RNs—either greeted Luke with a smile or nodded in respect. Leilani couldn't help noting that several of them eyed her with curiosity.

When they reached the cafeteria, he led her to the buffet, then grabbed a couple of trays, one for each of them. He started by taking an extra-large glass of orange juice for himself and offering her one.

"No thanks."

"By the way," he said, "the breakfast burritos are really good. And filling."

"That's nice to know, but I'm just going to have tea and a bagel."

As if she'd never said a word, he picked up a bowl of fruit and placed it on her tray. "If you're going to hang out here, sleeping on chairs, you'll need something more substantial than that to eat."

In the past, Luke had always been assertive with

his friends, but he'd seemed to tiptoe around her, letting her call the shots. Apparently, that wasn't the case any longer.

He poured himself a large coffee and waited while she chose an herbal tea bag and filled a cup with hot water. And when they reached the breakfast food that had been placed under warm lights, he took a burrito. "Are you sure I can't tempt you with this?"

He'd always tempted her—in more ways than one. But they were adults now, older and wiser. And with a past that separated them rather than bonded them together.

"I'm sure," she said.

When they reached the cashier, he tried to pay, but she refused to let him do so. For some reason, it had seemed too much like a date, too reminiscent of days gone by. And quite frankly, she preferred they keep a respectful distance.

Luke led her to a corner table in the rear of the room where they took a seat. So much had changed, yet the past hung over them like a black storm cloud that threatened to burst in an angry downpour.

Her brother, Kami, had only been fourteen when he'd died, run down in the middle of the street by drug dealers. Had Luke not broken his promise, Kami would have been home and safely tucked in bed.

And Leilani still would have him.

But she'd be darned if she'd mention anything that would open up a conversation about the tragedy that tore them apart. Or the fact that Luke had not only led her brother astray, but led him to his death.

Instead, she broached the subject of Carrie's baby boy. "Dr. Gray is trying to ward off contractions until the medication that assists lung development kicks in."

"At this point, each day in the womb makes a big difference," Luke said.

"Do they know whether he suffered any brain damage during the beating?"

"The initial ultrasound looks good," he said, as though unwilling to discuss the possibility.

She watched as he opened his burrito, spooned in a load of salsa, then rewrapped it and took a hearty bite.

"And what about Carrie?" she asked.

"It's still touch and go right now."

They ate quietly for a while, which should have been comforting. But for some reason, the silence was unsettling, and she felt compelled to fill the void.

"They arrested Joel Graves," she said. "The perp."

"Good." Luke took a thirsty swig of juice. "It was a brutal beating, and he was obviously out of control. Why did he tear into her like that?"

"Jealousy," she said.

"Sounds like she made a bad choice of boyfriends."

"Carrie grew up in a dysfunctional home," Leilani explained. "And her parents abused her. She ran away when she was sixteen and married a guy who ended up beating her, too. She entered a battered womens' shelter in Los Angeles a few years back, got counseling, took some college courses, and relocated to Phoenix. But while she was there, she got involved with Joel and soon learned that he was prone to violence."

"Sounds like she'd be better off remaining single," Luke said.

"She recently came to that conclusion, too."

He took another drink of orange juice, nearly finishing the glass. "If Carrie was living in Phoenix, what was she doing in San Diego?"

"She works for an advertising agency and had a chance to transfer. She'd broken up with Joel, but suspected that he wasn't happy about the split. So she used the opportunity to put some distance between them. For a while it appeared that he'd accepted that the relationship was over. But apparently, he got wind of her pregnancy and that really set him off."

"Is the baby his?" Luke asked.

"No. And she wasn't cheating on him, either. She went to a sperm bank."

When Luke didn't comment, she let the subject drop.

"How'd you meet her?" he asked.

"I'm a social worker and counseled her at the shelter in L.A."

In fact, Carrie had been her first project. No, that's not true. *Luke* had been her first project.

At one time, and for the past twelve years, she'd thought she'd failed with him. But maybe not. It's possible that he'd taken to heart some of the things she'd told him.

"It's a good profession for you to pursue," he

said. "You always did have a thing for strays and underdogs."

She supposed that was a result of growing up in the home of a minister and his wife. But Luke's turn-around hadn't been as easy to see coming.

"What about you?" she asked. "What made you decide to go to medical school?"

It wasn't a tough question, but Luke wasn't sure how honest he wanted to be.

Her brother's death had been influential—but in a negative way. After Kami died, Leilani and her family blamed him. And when she returned to Hawaii for the funeral, she never came back to San Diego, never contacted him. Never answered his calls.

The guilt and grief threatened to destroy him, so he'd easily fallen back into his old lifestyle to escape. Only the drinking, carousing and fighting became worse than ever before.

Did he want Leilani to know all of that?

Did he want her to realize she and her family had been right about him all along?

He let out a breath he hadn't realized he'd been holding. "One night, I met a police detective named Harry Logan. The guy has a real knack with hard-ass kids and saw something promising in me. He took me under his wing, encouraged me to go back to school, then helped me get a job at a hospital. Medicine fascinated me, and I decided to become a doctor."

"Harry must be a special guy."

"He is. And there are quite a few young men in

and around the San Diego area who consider him the father they never had."

Luke was one of them.

His real dad had been an alcoholic college professor and had run off with a graduate student when Luke was just a kid. And his mom had never been able to recover from the emotional blow. At least not while he'd been in his formative years and could have used a functional parent in his corner.

He'd loved his mom—and the fact that he'd failed her when she'd needed him most would haunt him for the rest of his days. But when he was a kid, she seemed to think she was the only one who'd been abandoned and was hurting, so he'd found it easier to avoid going home.

By the time he'd become a teenager, they had moved to a run-down apartment in the inner city—not far from where Leilani's aunt lived. And with no one to encourage him or keep him in line, he began hanging out with the wrong crowd.

Luke might have been a natural-born rebel, but he suspected that having a half-decent father probably would have kept him from getting into too much trouble.

When he met Leilani, she was a college-bound senior who'd recently moved in with her aunt. And his hormones had done what the teachers hadn't been able to—got him to knuckle down and study.

Had Kami not died, Luke might have become a doctor anyway—because of Leilani's influence.

She'd believed in him and had made him want to be the kind of guy she could respect.

"Having a father to look up to is important for a boy," she said now, obviously thinking about the baby her friend was carrying.

Leilani had always been compassionate, always concerned with the feelings of others. And Luke could see the grief and worry etched on her face.

He reached across the table and placed his hand on hers. "You can't get personally involved like this. It'll drag you under if you let it."

Luke's touch sent a shiver of heat up Leilani's arm, and she nearly bolted. But before she could pull away or argue about her decision to get involved with Carrie or anyone else who reached out to her, Luke's name blasted over the intercom.

"Dr. Wynter, dial zero-five-six. Dr. Wynter, dial zero-five-six."

"Excuse me." He stood, then picked up his tray. "I need to take that."

Leilani watched him go, watched the way he swaggered out of the cafeteria with confidence and pride.

Just seeing him again had resurrected memories of what they'd once had and lost. What he'd thrown away by being negligent and acting carelessly.

When Kami died, she'd written Luke off as a delinquent, a lost soul. She now realized she'd been wrong. He'd managed to make something out of himself and earn a medical degree to boot. She ought to be happy for him, she supposed. And in a way, she was.

But that opened a whole new can of worms—night crawlers and squirmy critters sure to complicate her life and that of her son.

Seeing him again was a complication in itself, she supposed. A reminder of the secret she'd kept.

Danny had Leilani's tan complexion, her dark hair. But he had his father's eye color, a pretty emerald green. The shape, too. But more than that, he had Luke's mannerisms—the charming smile, the single dimple in his cheek when he cracked a joke.

As she finished her tea and picked at the melon in her fruit cup, a group of nurses entered the cafeteria. After snagging their breakfast from the buffet, they chose a table not far from hers.

She ignored them until Luke's name was mentioned.

"Guess who managed to get a date with Dr. Wynter last week," a pudgy blonde said.

"Who?" the group chimed in harmony.

"Tori Claypool."

"From the blood bank? How'd she do that?"

"Your guess is as good as mine. But apparently we're not the only ones eager to find out why he was nicknamed Hot Lips."

"You'd better be careful," the blonde said. "You wouldn't want to slip and call him that to his face. He doesn't seem to have a sense of humor when he's on duty, and I think Marge-the-Sarge is the only one who can get away with teasing him without making him angry."

"It's too bad he works nights and so many

weekends," a redhead added. "That's so limiting to a relationship."

"If you're talking about concerts and evening activities," the blonde said, "I'd be happy to spend a quiet afternoon at his place and show him the true meaning of a cheap date."

Obviously, Dr. Luke Wynter was not only the resident E.R. doctor, but the resident heartthrob as well.

When Leilani had been in high school and had been dating Luke, she'd heard similar conversations in the girls' locker room. She could understand why it would bother her then. But for some reason, she found a pang of jealousy even more unsettling now.

She tried to shrug it off and explain it away. After all, Luke was a handsome hunk who exuded raw sexuality. Obviously women still threw themselves at him.

While some things may have changed, others hadn't. Luke still played the field and had his choice of eager women who didn't mind being one of several.

Ready to escape the annoying chatter, as well as the green-eyed monster poking around in her chest, Leilani picked up her tray and put it on the shelf set aside for those that had been used. Then she grabbed her purse and headed for the lobby door.

She had better things to do than eavesdropping on a group of giggling post-adolescents. Besides, her car had been on the blink, so she and Danny had flown to San Diego. She'd had to borrow Addie's Taurus and hated to leave her aunt without a vehicle any longer than necessary. In addition to that, she was eager to see Danny.

Aunt Addie was looking after him, and when Leilani had called last night to check on them, she'd learned that they'd made popcorn and were watching television. She'd promised her son a trip to the zoo today, but now she'd have to postpone it until tomorrow.

It was tough disappointing him.

And if she ever decided to reveal the truth about his father, she'd *really* disappoint him. Not because of who Luke was.

But because of what she'd told the boy about him.

Leilani parked the car in the underground garage, then took the elevator up to her aunt's small apartment on the fourth floor and stepped into the hallway that bore the same blue plaid carpet she'd remembered. It was more worn than ever and, like everything else in the building, needed to be replaced.

Without any windows to air out the hallway, the scent of stale cigarette smoke had permeated drapes, walls and flooring.

At one time, the Eberly Arms Apartments hadn't been the safest complex. But it seemed as though the tenants, at least the ones on this floor, had all been around for a while. Most of them were her aunt's age and looked out for each other, which was comforting.

As she used her key and let herself inside, Danny jumped up from the sofa and rushed to meet her. "Mom, you're back. *Finally.* When are we leaving?"

Excitement spread over his face, and his green eyes—so much like his father's—glimmered.

She bit her lip, struggling to find words that wouldn't disappoint him too badly, but failed. Instead, she ran a loving hand through his brown hair and offered him a bone-weary smile. "Just let me take a quick shower, honey. Then we'll go. All right?"

His grin was worth the sacrifice of a few hours sleep.

As she started toward the guest bedroom she and Danny had been sharing, Aunt Addie stopped her. "Lani, you look dog-tired and ready to drop. Why did you agree to go to the zoo today? I'm sure Danny would understand your need for rest."

"I know. He's a good kid." She cast her elderly aunt a smile. "But this is supposed to be his vacation, too. He's really looking forward to visiting the reptile house and seeing the pythons and the rattlesnakes."

"I'm sure they'll be there tomorrow."

True, but Leilani also wanted her son to get some fresh air and sunshine. While she'd been gone, she'd asked her aunt not to take him outdoors. She had no idea what she'd do if anything happened to him. The thought of losing him like she'd lost Kami was too painful to contemplate.

"How's your friend Carrie doing?" Addie asked.

"She's hanging in there."

Addie clucked her tongue. "It's a downright shame what happened to her. She's better off without a man in her life anyway."

Leilani found it hard to argue, especially with a woman who refused to remarry after a nasty divorce, a woman who still seemed angry with Leilani's father for not allowing her to raise his children on the mainland.

But when Leilani's parents died, their will had been explicit. Leilani and Kami were to live with their maternal grandparents on Lanai—an island not far from Oahu, where they'd been living.

"I'm glad you finally learned that lesson," Addie said, as she opened the linen closet. She pulled out a blue towel and washcloth then handed them to Leilani.

"What lesson are you talking about?"

"That most men can't be trusted. You're better off this way."

Leilani wasn't quite sure what she meant. "Do you think that's why I never married?"

"Well, you've had bad experiences with two young men. First with that hellion who was responsible for Kami's death. Then that Navy SEAL who got you pregnant."

Leilani glanced down the hall, making sure Danny wasn't within hearing distance. "Danny's birth blessed this entire family, so his father did us all a favor. And for what it's worth, I've been too busy with work and trying to be a mother to my son to even think about dating. It has nothing to do with not trusting men."

"Hmph." Addie handed her the linens. "Nevertheless, I'm glad you haven't tried to find that boy a stepfather. He's doing just fine without one."

Was he?

She'd told herself Danny's father wasn't a man he

could look up to, a man he could trust. But now she wasn't so sure.

Of course, there were more reasons than that for keeping Danny a secret for eleven years.

First, she didn't know Luke anymore. What if he let her son down? Or made promises he wouldn't keep?

Second, she'd always preached the importance of honesty to her son. And the lie she'd told him about his father had been a whopper.

Perched on a hilltop that overlooked the Pacific, Oceana General Hospital was located about twenty minutes north of downtown San Diego. The large white stucco building had an old-world, Spanish style, with a flower-lined walkway and a stone-crafted water fountain bubbling at the entrance.

Luke liked the way the lights shined upon the water at night, which is why he chose to enter through the front door and not the emergency room.

After parking his SUV in the lot assigned to doctors, he pushed through the double glass doors into the lobby. He walked past the ladies dressed in pink who were members of the hospital auxiliary and headed down the walkway to the ICU. His shift would start soon, but he wanted to check on Carrie—again.

His interest in the beaten pregnant woman went against the grain, he supposed. Whenever any other cases had tugged at his frayed heartstrings, he'd always been able to successfully fight off the urge to get involved. So he didn't know why he hadn't done the same with this one.

Sure you do, an adolescent voice whispered.

He cursed under his breath. Okay, so it was Leilani who had the hold on him—her and that damn guilt he still carried.

Upon punching in the code that allowed him into the ICU, he proceeded to the nurses' station, where he learned that Carrie had been assigned to Bethany Paige, an attractive redhead he'd dated a while back. The shifts were about to change.

"How's Carrie Summers doing?" he asked.

Bethany arched a brow, obviously surprised to see him out of the E.R.

Okay, so it was common knowledge he didn't often follow up on a patient.

He shrugged. "Ms. Summers is a friend of a friend."

"Oh, yeah?" Bethany crossed her arms as though making some kind of assumption she had no business making. "Not much has changed. She's having some intermittent contractions, but nothing productive."

"Is she still unconscious?"

"Yes. There's been some brain swelling, but Dr. Wofford has been keeping a close eye on it."

"Good."

Bethany blew out a sigh. "I hope they put away the guy who did this to her for a long time."

"So do I."

The brief relationship he and Bethany had shared

was over, yet the memories, few that they were, filled the air between them.

"You know," she said, "I don't have any hard feelings about…well, you know."

Luke smiled. "I'm glad. You deserve someone who can commit and give you the white-picket-fence dream. I'm afraid I'm just a loner at heart, a guy who thrives on working nights and sleeping days."

"I'd thought maybe that might change—if you met the right woman."

He tugged gently at a red lock of hair. "I'm afraid it's too late for that. I'm too set in my ways."

"Yeah, well thanks for being honest and up-front about it. I appreciate that."

He let the curly strand go, losing the fleeting connection that reflected the intimacy they'd shared for a couple of weeks.

At first, Bethany had claimed she wanted a no-strings-attached affair, too. But as they spent more time together, she began to press for more, so Luke ended things.

Some men might have let it go on longer, but he'd learned a lot of things from Harry Logan, especially the meaning of integrity. Life was far less complicated when people were honest with each other.

"Will you mention to the night-duty nurse that I'd like to know if there's any change in her condition?"

Bethany nodded. "Sure."

Luke tossed her a thanks-for-understanding smile, then turned and left the ICU. He headed to the waiting room, where he expected to see Leilani. Maybe this time, he'd get a chance to tell her what he'd meant to say before.

When he paused in the doorway, he found her seated on the sofa, her shoes kicked off and on the floor, her bare feet tucked under her.

"Isn't it time for you to be heading home?" he asked.

At the sound of his voice, Leilani looked up, uncurled her legs and quickly slipped on her shoes. "Sorry. I got a bit too comfy."

"Good. You spend enough time here that you ought to make yourself at home." He shot her a grin. "In fact, why don't you come with me to the cafeteria? I've got a couple of minutes before I have to head to work."

"Thanks, but I can't." She tucked a strand of hair behind her ear. "I heard Dr. Wofford is going to be making his rounds soon, and I want to be here when he does."

Something rigid inside him warmed and waffled, and he took a seat beside her.

"Is this all normal?" Leilani asked.

Luke didn't want to tell her there was a chance Carrie wouldn't wake up. Leilani was worried enough, and he didn't want to add a stress about something that might not present itself.

He went on to explain some of the medical tests and treatments in layman terms. She seemed to appreciate the time he spent with her. More than once, he wanted to reach out to her, to take her hand, but he didn't want to force an intimacy they no longer had.

Luke had never gotten the chance to tell her how sorry he'd been that Kami had died. And a part of him wondered if he'd ever be able to find forgiveness in her eyes.

He could understand why he might not.

Her brother's death had been devastating, the details ugly. The poor kid had been young and as innocent as they came. When his death had been declared drug-related, it had cast a sordid cloud over his memory and had shamed his religious family.

Of course, Luke wouldn't bring any of that up now, not at the hospital. Instead he would drive by her aunt's house on his next day off and talk to her there.

Assuming, of course, that her aunt no longer had the shotgun she'd threatened to fire at him if he ever showed up at her door again.

Chapter Three

The next morning, when his shift ended, Luke stopped by the ICU again, and the fact that he did bothered him more than ever.

Why couldn't he let Leilani go?

Damned if he knew. He might be a doctor, but he sure as hell didn't know the first thing about curing a worn-out case of puppy love. Or whatever it was he still felt for his old lover.

Sympathy maybe?

A misplaced sense of loyalty?

After checking in on Carrie and hearing the latest, he went by the waiting room, only to see that Leilani wasn't there. A sense of disappointment settled over him, which he found even more annoying.

He ought to be happy she was taking care of herself and getting some rest. That's what *he* should be doing.

On the way out of the hospital, he walked through the lobby and kept his eyes peeled for Leilani on the outside chance she would be coming while he was going. And, much to his relief, he spotted her just outside the glass doors.

She wore a pale-yellow sweater and a pair of black jeans today. Her hair was loose and curled under at the shoulders. When she cast a friendly grin at the ladies dressed in matching pink smocks and seated at the information desk, greeting them warmly, he realized she was not only as lovely as ever, but she was just as kindhearted.

When her gaze landed on him, his pulse skipped a beat, then rumbled to life.

Strange how she could still have that effect on him.

As she drew nearer, he noted dark circles under her eyes.

"I was hoping you'd stayed home last night, but something tells me you didn't get much rest."

She shrugged a shoulder and offered him a shy hula-girl smile. "You're right. I didn't sleep well."

He wasn't sure where he wanted to go with that, since she was certainly able to determine her needs on her own. But neither could he completely ignore her statement. "Are you staying with your aunt?"

"Yes, we've been…" She cleared her throat. "I've been visiting her, and we've been catching up."

"Does she still live at the Eberly Arms? From what I remember, it used to get pretty loud there."

"It's not so bad anymore, but last night Aunt Addie had a spell that worried me. So I woke up periodically to check on her."

Unable to quell his curiosity—professional or otherwise—he asked, "What kind of spell?"

"She has diabetes and her blood sugar level dropped. It took me a while to figure out she needed a glass of orange juice."

"Is she under regular medical care?"

Leilani nodded. "Yes, but since I arrived I've noticed that she gets a little…forgetful sometimes. I'm afraid she might not be checking her sugar level regularly or taking her insulin properly. So I have her doctor's number and plan to give him a call once his office opens."

They stood there awhile, sexual attraction—at least on his part—buzzing and sparking like a high voltage wire downed by a storm. Her scent, something floral and springtime fresh, mingling with buzzing pheromones, drew him to her. He tried his best to ignore it, but he wasn't having any luck.

"Now I have another reason to stick around for a while," she said, "so I called my office this afternoon and requested a leave of absence. I'm going to stay with Aunt Addie until I can be sure she's following her doctor's orders and until Carrie recovers."

Luke didn't mention that the jury was still out on Carrie's full recovery. "By the way, I'm not sure if you've heard. Her boyfriend was arraigned and charged with attempted murder."

"I'm glad to hear it."

"There's also been talk about taking the baby early," Luke added, revealing what he'd learned earlier.

"Have they scheduled the birth?"

"No. They're still waiting. At this point, each day the baby stays in the womb, the better chance he has."

"I told you that Carrie asked me to look after him if something…happened to her." Leilani tucked a strand of hair behind her ear, revealing a pearl earring much like June Cleaver would have worn.

"You'll make a great mom," he told her, meaning every word.

Her lips parted as though she meant to respond, then she clamped them shut.

"How about a cup of coffee?" he asked. "Maybe breakfast?"

"No thanks. I'd better pass. Besides, your fan club probably doesn't need to see us together."

He shifted his weight to one foot and crossed his arms. "What are you talking about?"

Something that resembled humor glimmered in her eyes. "Several of the nurses think you're pretty hot. And they're eager to join the ranks of your notable conquests."

He was aware of that, but for some reason it embarrassed him to have Leilani privy to idle chat, speculation and rumor. "I don't make a habit of dating the women I work with."

The humor disappeared from her gaze, and skepticism took its place. "Oh no?"

He doubted Bethany had been talking to anyone. The reason he'd dated her in the first place had to do with her ability to be discreet and the fact she didn't seem to play the games some of the others did. "If there's been talk, it's not true."

"Aw, come on, Luke." She crossed her arms, facing off with him in a way that made her appear a lot taller than her five-foot-four stature. "I'm not buying that."

"Why not?"

"I've kissed you before, Doctor. And I have every reason to believe your nickname wasn't fabricated."

Feeling both flattered and called on the carpet at the same time, he arched a brow. "My nickname?"

"Hot Lips." Then she uncrossed her arms and swept through the lobby, leaving him to ponder the heated, breath-stealing kisses they used to share.

And the fact she didn't believe he'd lost his touch.

The next day Luke was off duty. After getting his minimum required sleep, he made a call to the hospital and managed to get Leilani's cell number, which she'd left as a contact on Carrie's chart.

He hoped to convince her to have dinner with him that evening. Nothing fancy. Maybe someplace by the ocean, where they could sit outside and watch the waves roll in. He did his best thinking outdoors, where walls didn't close in on him.

A seaside café is also romantic, a small voice whispered.

Too damn bad, he answered. He wasn't going to try and impress her with candles and wine. He just needed to talk to her—out in the open air. And far from a hospital setting.

If Kami crept into the conversation, so be it. It was time for her to hear Luke's side of the story. To realize he hadn't meant for any of it to happen.

But when he dialed her number, her voice mail answered on the first ring, which made him suspect she'd turned off her cell.

Odd.

He showered, shaved and threw on a pair of jeans and a light blue button-down shirt. All the while, he struggled with the idea of just showing up at her aunt's place and talking to her in person.

An hour later, he gave up the fight and drove to Eberly Arms Apartments, where Leilani had said she was staying. Once he parked his black Expedition in the garage, he took the elevator up to the fourth floor. It might have been twelve years, but he still remembered exactly where her aunt lived.

Apartment 4-E.

The building hadn't changed much, just grown faded and run-down. It was quiet though. No one loitering in the halls.

He pushed the bell, although he didn't hear a buzz or a ring. So he followed it with a knock, then waited for someone to answer.

God, he hoped it was Leilani. Her aunt had never made any bones about her low opinion of him—even before Kami died—so he wasn't looking forward to seeing her now.

The door opened, revealing a dark-haired boy who appeared to be about twelve.

Oops. Maybe the old memory wasn't as good as he thought it was. He glanced at the number on the door. He could have sworn it was 4-E. Leilani had mentioned her aunt lived in the same place, but maybe she'd moved into another apartment in the complex.

"I'm looking for Leilani Stephens," he told the boy. "Is she staying here?"

"Yeah." The boy turned and yelled into the living room. "Mom, some guy wants to talk to you!"

Mom?

Although stunned, Luke couldn't help scanning the kid from the top of his dark brown hair to the white socks on his feet.

Leilani hadn't said squat about having a kid. And the fact that this one was about eleven or twelve set off all kinds of bells and whistles in Luke's brain.

"Yes?" Leilani entered the room and approached the door. When their gazes met, recognition dawned and her face paled.

She was obviously surprised to see him, but something else in her expression suggested that his calculations weren't far off the mark.

He again studied the boy, trying to look beyond the white T-shirt and blue board shorts to spot something familiar, something genetic Luke may have contributed.

His complexion, while more fair than Leilani's, still bore evidence of her Hawaiian roots. His hair was brown and lighter than hers, but not by much.

Luke didn't find anything revealing, other than a pair of green eyes—which were sizing up the adults who stood gawking at each other in the doorway.

"Your mom and I used to be friends a long time ago," he explained to the boy—his son? "I'm Luke Wynter. What's your name?"

"Danny."

Luke nodded. "And let me guess. You're probably about…eleven years old."

"Yeah."

"I must be psychic," Luke said, "and I'm guessing that your birthday is in April."

"Hey, you're pretty good. It's April tenth."

Reality was closing in on him in a cold, hard rush. And he'd be damned if he knew what to do about it.

Leilani had some explaining to do.

"I came by to ask your mom if she'd like to go to dinner with me." Luke's gaze traveled from the boy to his mother. "But now that I'm here…I don't think I'll give you that much of an option, Leilani. We *need* to talk. At dinner or outside."

She didn't respond right away, but needless to say, she'd been blindsided to see him standing at the door. Just as blindsided as Luke had been when Danny answered his knock.

"Is your car parked in the garage?" she asked.

"Yes. Just outside the elevator."

"Give me a few minutes. I'll ask Aunt Addie to look after Danny, grab my purse and meet you down there."

"All right."

Then she slowly closed the door, leaving Luke to head for the garage.

The place where he used to wait for her when they were teenagers and her aunt hadn't approved of him.

The soles of Luke's loafers crunched on the oil-stained concrete floor as he paced the underground parking garage, where the dank odor of gasoline fumes and exhaust was an unwelcome reminder of days gone by.

Fortunately, he didn't have to wait long.

When Leilani exited the elevator and joined him in the garage, he opened the passenger door of his Ford Expedition and gestured for her to climb inside. Then he headed west, toward the ocean, where the air was fresh and clean.

Leilani, who'd not only grabbed her purse, but had changed her clothes and put on some lipstick, sat beside him as sober and quiet as a cloistered nun.

The seconds stretched between them like a rubber band that had seen better days, and he waited for the snap. The sting. But apparently they were both hesitant to broach the subject they needed to discuss, the questions he wanted answered.

Did you bear my child?

Why didn't you tell me?
Where do we go from here?

He wanted to press her, yet needed time to assimilate the possibility, the ramifications, the future.

But it was the past that came to mind, the memory of the first and only time they'd made love. The night they'd conceived a child.

It had happened at the beach one moonlit evening in July, when their kisses had gotten too hot to ignore, their passion too strong to deny. She'd wanted it nearly as badly as he did, and he'd been nervous and afraid. He'd feared that he would hurt her somehow and worried that she'd regret it afterward.

Leilani had been a virgin, and although Luke had already slept with several girls, he'd come to realize there was a big difference between sex and making love.

He'd never experienced anything as sweet as running his hands along her body and claiming her as his own. He'd taken his time and tried to make it special for her. Special for both of them, he realized, because he hadn't been blessed with anything as innocent or as emotionally moving since and doubted he ever would.

She'd cried afterward, which had torn him apart, but she'd sworn everything was okay, that she was just overwhelmed by it all. While removing the condom, he suspected it might have sprung a slight leak, but hadn't wanted to frighten her or cause her any more tears. So he'd kept his mouth shut.

More than ever, he'd been filled with the need to

protect her forever. But forever hadn't been in their cards. And days later, when her brother died, he'd realized how lousy he was at looking after anyone other than himself.

After pulling into a parking space at the side of the restaurant and shutting off the ignition, he couldn't keep quiet any longer. "Is Danny my son?"

She glanced down in her lap and fiddled with the garnet ring, then caught his gaze. "Yes."

The simple answer bombarded him with shock, hurt and anger, but he fought the urge to respond. He was afraid of what he might say or offer.

Leilani had enough to hold against him. A misguided comment now might open a Pandora's box of emotion, so he merely nodded, then climbed from the vehicle, realizing his life was becoming complicated in ways he couldn't quite grasp.

Before he could open the door for her, she exited and headed for the entrance of the small restaurant that had become a favorite of locals.

Once inside, he asked to be seated on the patio and away from the other diners. The hostess obliged, escorting them to an outdoor table, where he caught the heady scent of a sea breeze and could see and hear the waves crash upon the shore. It was cool tonight, but portable heaters stood ready to keep them comfortable.

He was neither hot nor cold, yet his nerves were raw and he was as skittish as a stray cat in a rock-filled gunnysack being hurled off the dock.

Since Leilani wasn't quick to offer any explanations or a confession, he brought up the subject himself. "Why didn't you tell me?"

She didn't respond right away, nor did she need to.

The whole Kami thing elbowed into the forefront, settled over them and provided the answers to all his questions.

She'd been too angry with him at first, too devastated by her loss. But he also suspected it had something to do with the grandparents who'd raised her, a conservative minister and his wife who lived on a small Hawaiian island.

"I know we didn't part on good terms," he said, "but that's not the point. You shouldn't have had to go through a pregnancy alone."

"I didn't. My grandmother was with me. And she was very supportive."

"That's not the same." Luke had a ton of experience in obstetrics now. Back then he would have been scared spitless, but he would have done right by her. "You should have called me."

"It crossed my mind," she admitted. "But I decided it would be easier not to."

"Easier for who?"

"Me. My family." The wind whipped a strand of hair across her face, and she tucked it behind her ear. "And for Danny."

"Why?"

"You were prone to trouble back then. And you gave me no reason to believe you would be responsible or that you would be good daddy material."

She had a point. And he wasn't sure that he was daddy material now. But that didn't mean he wanted to leave a kid of his to fend for himself, without any paternal influence or guidance. And like it or not, he *had* fathered a child. A son who'd spent the first eleven years of his life with a single mother.

"Besides," she added, "you didn't want to be a father."

He didn't. But hell, that was before knowing he actually had a son.

What kind of loser did she think he was? One who was every bit as irresponsible as his own old man?

A myriad of emotions buzzed around in his head—surprise and anger, to name a couple.

"All right, I'll admit this is a bit mind-boggling. And I'm going to need some time to think about the logistics of it all." He'd have to make some adjustments in his life if Danny was going to become a part of it. And whether Leilani—*or her aunt*—liked it or not, he *was* going to be a father to the boy.

At least as much as he was able.

"I could use some time to get used to all of this, too," she said. "And to figure out what I'm going to tell Danny."

"What's so hard about telling him he has a father who is willing to support him and be there for him?"

She bit her lip and glanced down at the table, finding her hand and fingering the heirloom ring. Then she glanced up, her expression solemn.

"Because Danny thinks you're dead."

Chapter Four

"You told him I died?" Luke's voice rose above the roar of the waves crashing on the sand.

Leilani didn't want to discuss the past or defend her decision, but that didn't appear to be an option right now. "I did what I thought was best at the time."

He opened his mouth to speak—or maybe to object—then snapped it shut. She imagined him counting to ten, trying to gain control of his temper.

Had he mellowed with age? As a teenager, he'd been quick to react with anger, which often led to physical altercations and, as a result, trouble with teachers or other authority figures.

"You thought my son would be better off thinking I was dead?" he finally asked.

"Back then? Yes."

"Why?"

"I thought that would be better than knowing his father hadn't wanted him."

"What are you talking about? You never even gave me a chance."

She fingered the napkin in front of her, finding it difficult to look him in the eyes, although, if she had it all to do over again, she'd make the same decision.

Or would she?

It was hard to say. If she'd known that Luke was going to do something positive with his life, she might have contacted him. But there hadn't been a crystal ball handy.

Obviously Luke was no longer the young man she'd once known. Neither was he the convict she'd imagined he would become. And that made him a complete stranger now.

"You should have told me." His eyes bored into her, stirring up dissonance about the decision she'd made. "At least you had a way to contact *me*."

Yes. And he hadn't known how to find her. Not without her aunt's cooperation, which he never would have gotten.

"You may not remember this," she said, her gaze meeting his. "But one day, I heard a rumor about one of the girls you'd dated."

Leilani hadn't been the only teenage girl who found Luke appealing. He'd had a legion of others wanting to go out with him, many of whom had been eager to give themselves to him. And, according to rumor, several had.

"What about her?" he asked.

"Her name was Connie, and she was pregnant. Some of the girls in health class said the baby was yours. When I asked you if it was true, you said no."

"I was always careful."

The fact that he hadn't been careful enough on at least one occasion hovered over them, but neither commented.

"Do you remember what else you told me?" she asked, fingering the rolled edge of the napkin in front of her.

"No."

"You said, 'No way. I don't want kids and would never let that happen.'"

His eyes, green and calculating, locked in on her. "What's your point?"

"I had every reason to believe you wouldn't have wanted Danny."

"You're right. I didn't want kids back then. My home life was the pits, and I didn't harbor any delusions of a better future. But that doesn't mean I wouldn't have stepped up to the plate. Nor does it mean I don't want to be a part of Danny's life—now that I know he exists."

"I can understand that." Her decision had been based upon the knowledge at hand. She'd also been struggling with grief at the time, but she didn't want to broach that subject or the fact that she still blamed

Luke for her little brother's death—a loss that still haunted her.

Kami would be twenty-six now, out of college and pursuing a career. Maybe he'd even be married.

Instead, thanks to Luke's recklessness, he was buried on the island of Lanai. And grief still dogged her when she thought about him in that satin-lined casket, his bright-eyed smile gone forever.

Kami had also been her lone connection to her parents, and when he died it was like losing them all over again.

"I wish you would have trusted me to do right by you," Luke said.

"I was young. Remember?" And she'd also been naive. Raised by conservative grandparents, Leilani had been sheltered and protected until she'd turned seventeen and was sent to San Diego to live with Aunt Addie and finish her senior year.

Talk about culture shock.

She'd done her best to focus on her schoolwork, something that had always been a priority. And she'd managed to maintain a 4.0 grade point average, even though the neighborhood boys were fascinated by her and often found innovative ways in which to interfere with her studies. For the most part, she'd ignored them all—until Luke caught her eye and turned her heart inside out.

"You loved me once," he said. "At least you said you did."

She *had* loved him. But, looking back, she suspected she'd also been enamored by his dark and dangerous edge. Leilani, a good girl in the classic sense, had been drawn to the known troublemaker, giving real credence to the "opposites attract" philosophy.

He'd also been a whiz in science and math and had been able to tutor her in chemistry. And one thing led to another.

In the distance, a seagull cried. She'd always considered it a sad and lonely sound, but found it even more so today.

"I did love you," she finally admitted.

He reached a hand across the table, placing it over top of hers, stilling the movements of her fingers as they tore at the napkin.

The warmth of his touch shot a shiver of heat through her blood, and the intensity in his gaze sent her heart skittering through her chest.

It was impossible to deny that she was still attracted to him. And in spite of all the choices she'd made in the past and her efforts to distance herself from him emotionally, there remained a connection—their son, a little boy who thought his father was dead and believed his mother valued honesty above all else.

"You need to tell him the truth," Luke said. "I want to be a part of his life."

She'd been afraid of that. "It's a little more complicated than that."

"Then uncomplicate it."

"It's not that easy."

After Kami's funeral, Leilani had remained in the islands until it was time to fly to Los Angeles and begin college. But just days before she was to leave, she learned she was going to have Luke's baby.

The hardest thing she'd ever had to do was to tell her grandparents that she was unwed and pregnant, that she'd failed to listen to their instructions about sexual purity and abstinence. But there'd been no way on God's earth that she could have slapped them with the ultimate betrayal and admit that the hellion who'd been responsible for Kami's death was also the father of her illegitimate baby. It would have completely crushed them. So she'd made up a fictitious ex-boyfriend, saying he'd joined the Navy and shipped out to parts unknown.

They'd been terribly disappointed, but when Danny was born, they saw him as a precious gift and were quick to forgive.

"You've always been honest," Luke said. "I can't imagine you wanting to keep this secret. Not anymore."

That was the problem. How was she supposed to tell her family—especially her son—that she'd lied? That she wasn't as honest as she'd led them all to believe?

"I'll tell him," she said. "I'll tell everyone." And she *would*. "Just give me some time."

"How long do you need?"

"I don't know." She was a social worker. Problem solving and communications skills came easy to her. So did discussions about understanding and forgiveness. But in this case, she was too involved. Of course, she also had to admit that she wasn't ready to share Danny with his father yet.

Or to trust Luke to do right by the boy, to keep him safe.

They sat in silence for a while, the only noise the rumbling tide and the occasional cry of a gull. And when the waitress came by with two glasses of ice water and took their orders, Leilani was relieved to have an interruption, a reprieve from her thoughts.

Luke asked for a burger and a beer, while Leilani chose a diet soda. She passed on food, saying she wasn't hungry, when in truth, she feared it wouldn't sit well.

When the waitress went inside, Luke broke the silence. "I imagine your pregnancy put a damper on your college plans."

"For a while. When Danny was two, I registered him at a campus daycare facility, then pursued a degree in social work, as well as my master's. I had a few connections in the area, so I decided to stay in L.A., where I became a counselor at a battered women's shelter. You know the rest."

The hell I do, Luke wanted to snap, followed by a few choice swearwords. He didn't know jack about the last eleven years of his son's life. And he didn't want Leilani to give him an "in a nutshell" version. He wanted to know everything, like what foods he liked to eat. What games he liked to play. Who were his heroes? What did he do for fun?

Luke's cell phone vibrated, alerting him to a call. If he could have ignored it, he would have. But he needed to check the number on the display to make sure it wasn't the hospital. They were shorthanded in the E.R. today, and he was on call.

Nothing else was important enough to interrupt this conversation.

Scratch that, he thought, as he recognized Harry Logan's number. "Excuse me, I have to take this, but I'll make it quick."

She nodded, probably relieved to have a break from the hot seat she was sitting in, then took a sip of water.

Luke flipped open the phone and answered. "Hi, Harry. What did you find out?"

The man responsible for turning Luke's life around had been concerned about his wife's health, and Luke had been worried, too.

"We just got the biopsy results back," Harry said, "and that enlarged lymph gland was benign."

"That's great, Harry. I couldn't be happier for you."

"We're celebrating by having brunch tomorrow morning," Harry added. "Kay and I hope you can make it."

Luke glanced at Leilani, saw her fiddling with the napkin again, fraying the curled edges. Harry and his wife were always hosting barbecues and beach parties. And most of the guys who were referred to as Logan's Heroes showed up, sometimes bringing guests.

Luke always went stag.

"Are there going to be any kids there?" Luke asked.

"Several," Harry said. "Why? Do you have any you'd like to bring?"

Yeah. His son.

"Maybe." Luke looked at Leilani. "I need to talk to his mother and call you back."

When the line disconnected, Luke returned his cell phone to the clip on his belt. "That was my friend, Harry Logan. He's the retired detective who took me under his wing and encouraged me to make something out of my life."

"He sounds like a nice man."

"He's the greatest. He's been like a father to me, and I consider him my best friend. Anyway, he and his wife are having a brunch tomorrow morning, and I'd like to take you and Danny."

"Why?"

"I want to introduce my son to the Logans and my other friends." But it was more than that. The older couple and the other former delinquents had become family to him.

Leilani shook her head. "I'm not ready to make an announcement like that yet."

"When will you be ready?"

"I'm not sure. But soon."

Luke wasn't used to being put off, not at work or at play. But he'd bide his time. For a while.

"All right. I'll respect your wishes. If you'll join me, I'll tell everyone you're an old friend. They don't

need to know that we used to be involved or that
Danny is my son."

My son.

As often as Luke had told himself he didn't want
kids, the idea wasn't as wild or scary as he'd thought
it would be.

"So what do you say?" he asked. "It'll be a way
for Danny and me to get to know each other without
the awkwardness of our biological relationship
hovering over us."

She paused for the longest time, reminding him
that patience may be a virtue, but it wasn't one he
could claim. "All right. We'll go with you."

"Good." He settled into his seat, feeling as though
he'd taken a big step forward.

"Why don't you give us directions," she said.
"We'll meet you there."

So much for the forward momentum.

Her suggestion just set him back two steps.

The next morning, at a quarter-to-ten, Luke parked
his Expedition along the curb of Bayside Drive, in
front of the Logans' white Cape Cod-style house. He
remained in the vehicle, waiting for Leilani and
Danny to show up, hoping she hadn't reneged on her
agreement. It was important for her to come.

He'd extended the invitation for more reasons than
the one he'd given her, something he'd realized after
they'd had that awkward conversation and he'd
dropped her off at her aunt's house.

She'd been right to be concerned about him when he was younger, and he couldn't blame her for thinking he would end up in jail or worse. As an adolescent with a canyon-sized chip on his shoulder, Luke had made some bad choices and had been on a downhill slide, especially after he and Leilani had split up. But Harry had zeroed in on Luke's pain, seen through his bullshit and drawn him into the folds of his extended family, the likes of which Luke had never known before.

By inviting Leilani to come to the brunch, Luke hoped that when she met the Logans and spent time with the people who cared about him, she'd realize that he'd traded in his black hat for a white one—permanently.

If she could see that he was respectable now, both in and out of the hospital, maybe she'd feel better about telling Danny he had a father he could be proud of. And maybe—*just maybe*—she'd feel better about Luke as a man.

He'd give anything to know she no longer held him responsible for Kami's death.

As a white sedan slowed in front of Harry's house, and Luke spotted Leilani in the driver's seat, something warm rumbled through his chest, scrambling to gain a foothold. He did his best to shrug it off as he climbed from his SUV and strode toward the vehicle where Danny sat in the back seat.

Having a son was going to take some getting used to. It would also take some concentrated effort not to gawk or gape at the poor kid or to come across as an interrogator trying to learn everything he should know in a matter of minutes.

"Thanks for coming," he said to Leilani, as she climbed from the car in a pale-yellow sundress and a pair of white sandals.

The morning sun glistened on the strands of her silky black hair, like it did when she used to wear it waist-length. The years had been good to her. Damn good.

"I almost called you earlier," she began.

He didn't let her finish. "If it was to cancel, I'm glad you didn't. You're going to have a good time, I promise. The Logans are great people."

"Are there going to be kids here?" Danny asked as he opened the passenger door and slid out of the sedan.

"There sure are," Luke said. "Some of them are babies, a couple are about your age, but most are big kids like me."

Danny grinned, displaying a pair of dimples that reminded Luke of a couple he'd seen a time or two— in the mirror. It made him wonder what else they shared, but he'd take it slow and easy, respecting Leilani's wishes.

As they paused before the front door, Luke rang the bell, and moments later Kay Logan answered.

Harry's wife was an attractive rosy-cheeked woman with auburn hair. She smiled warmly and gave Luke a big hug. "I'm delighted you could make it. And that you brought friends."

"It's great to be able to celebrate your good health. I'm glad the biopsy came back negative."

"So are we," Kay said. "Thank you for answering all of our questions when we hated to bother Dr. Thompson at all hours of the night. Too bad you're not in private practice. Harry and I would be your first patients."

Luke winked. "If I ever decide to give up the pace and excitement of the E.R., I'll let you know."

After introducing Leilani to Kay, Luke placed his hand on their son's shoulder. "And this is Danny."

"Please come in." Kay stepped aside, allowing them in. "When it comes to get-togethers, Harry and I have a more-the-merrier philosophy."

That's for sure. The Logans were practically famous for their hospitality, at least with the one-time delinquents who credited Harry for being instrumental in convincing them to turn from their bad-ass ways.

The petite, older woman led them into the kitchen, a large room with white countertops and appliances.

"You have a lovely home," Leilani said.

"Thank you. We entertain a lot, so it works for us." Kay pointed to the small table in a sitting area, with lavender walls and a strip of violet-laced wallpaper trim along the ceiling. "Why don't you have a seat while I fix you a cup of coffee or tea."

Leilani complied, glancing first at a white plant stand that held several potted violets, then out the big bay window that revealed a lush lawn and colorful flowerbeds.

"You have a beautiful yard, too," Leilani told Kay, before turning to face the kitchen.

"Thank you. In fact, Harry and I thought it would be nice to eat outdoors."

"Speaking of Harry," Luke said, "where is he?"

"We had a late start this morning. We were called to the hospital just after seven o'clock to speak to a woman facing open heart surgery. So right now Harry is setting up tables in the backyard."

"Harry had bypass surgery a few years ago," Luke explained to Leilani. "The procedure is becoming fairly routine, but his case was complicated by other health conditions. Now the hospital asks him to talk to patients who are facing similar situations and are reluctant or nervous about what to expect."

"I'm sure your volunteerism is appreciated by everyone involved," Leilani said.

"That's true. The surgeons prefer their patients to have a positive attitude." Luke turned his attention to his son. "Hey, Danny. Since none of the other guys are here yet, why don't you and I help Harry with those tables?"

The boy nodded, then followed Luke outside.

Once the women were alone, Kay offered Leilani her choice of beverages, including fresh-squeezed orange juice.

"I'll have coffee," Leilani said. "Thank you."

"Where did you meet Luke?" Kay asked, as she

fixed two cups and set them on the table, next to the creamer and sugar bowl.

On the way over, Danny had asked her a similar question, and she'd gotten the impression that he thought there was a romance brewing between them. He'd almost seemed...supportive of her finding someone special.

Of course, she hadn't wanted him to get the wrong idea. Nor had she wanted to reveal too much too soon, so she'd told him that she and Luke had been old friends from school. And that they'd recently run into each other.

That was the same response and explanation she would offer Kay. "Luke and I met when we were seniors in high school and hadn't seen each other in years. Then, a couple of nights ago, we ran into each other again at Oceana General."

"Are you in the medical field, too?" Kay asked, taking a seat across the table.

"No, I'm not." Normally Leilani didn't go into details about her work with victims, but for some reason—Kay's position as a counselor at the hospital, she supposed—she felt compelled to explain. "My friend suffered a severe beating by an ex-boyfriend, and I followed the ambulance to the hospital."

"I'm sorry to hear that," Kay said. "I volunteer at Casa de Paz, a local womens' shelter. If there's anything I can do or any referrals I can make, I'd be happy to help."

"Thanks for the offer," Leilani said. "I work at a

shelter in Los Angeles, so I have a few connections, too. I just hope she recovers. And that her baby is okay. She's seven months pregnant."

"Oh, how sad." Compassion, as sincere as any Leilani had ever seen, washed across Kay's face. "I'll pray for them both. In fact, I'll call my church and put them on the prayer chain. It merely takes a call to the leader, and within minutes forty or more heartfelt requests will be Heaven-bound."

"I'd appreciate that. Her name is Carrie. She's still in a coma and threatening to go into premature labor."

Moments later, the call had been made that would set off a flurry of prayers, asking for healing and a safe delivery of the baby.

"You mentioned that Carrie was a friend," Kay said. "It must make it even more difficult to deal with something like this when you have an emotional bond with the victim."

"It does. Each of the women and children who passed through the portals of the safe house have touched me in one way or another, but Carrie was different. She became one of the shelter's top success stories. And over time she also became a friend."

"We have some admirable women, too. It's heartwarming to see them get back on their feet and take control of their lives again." Kay took a sip of coffee. "I'm sorry that Carrie didn't escape her abuser."

"Actually," Leilani said, "she made a complete break from the original guy. After leaving the shelter and taking some college courses, she relocated to a

Phoenix suburb, where she got a job and started dating. But when Joel Graves, the new man in her life, became controlling and had several violent outbursts, she feared he would become abusive, so she broke up with him and moved to San Diego."

"And he followed her?"

"Not right away." Leilani reached for her cup. "She'd been in town and settled for nearly a year. Two weeks ago she called and asked me to come and visit, to see her new place, a condo she'd purchased in Harbor Haven. She'd never sounded happier and was optimistic about the future."

"And Joel tracked her down?" Kay asked.

"She'd thought they'd made a clean break, that he'd gotten on with his life. But apparently that wasn't the case."

"I hope he's been arrested," Kay said, "and that they prosecute him to the fullest extent of the law."

"He's in jail and facing attempted murder charges."

"That's good to know," Kay said. "How are you holding up?"

"I'm fine—*now.*"

Kay didn't quiz her, but there was something about the maternal redhead that reminded Leilani of her grandmother, another woman of faith. And for some reason, it was easy to connect with Kay, to open up.

"Carrie and I had met earlier that day, and she'd shared her good news about the baby." Leilani lifted the china cup and savored a taste of the fresh brew. "Then, later that evening, she called me—frantic. Joel had somehow found her and when he realized she was pregnant he began banging on the door, demanding she let him in. She knew enough to call 911 first."

"Did you go to her?" Kay asked.

"Yes, I did." And just as she'd done so often in the past, Leilani had left Danny in the care of someone she trusted—Aunt Addie, this time—then drove as fast as was legal.

The memory stirred, drawing her mind back to the call, the terror in Carrie's voice, the ominous pounding on the door, the muffled shout of an angry man outside the house.

Glass shattered and Carrie screamed.

"You cheated on me!" the man yelled.

"No, I didn't."

"Damn it! Who is he?"

"There isn't anyone else, Joel. There never was. Please, let's sit down and talk about this."

"Talk?" Something large and heavy crashed against a wall or onto the floor. "You want to talk *now?* Hell, after we broke up, you never called me, never left me a phone number or anything. And when I checked with your old landlord, you left no forwarding address." The man—Joel—cursed and called her a derogatory name.

Leilani, who'd kept the cell phone line open as she'd began the drive to Harbor Haven, hoped she could get to the condo in time, although she prayed the police arrived first.

She'd confronted more than her share of abusers in the past, but it was usually after a beating—not during.

While she maneuvered through traffic and headed for Interstate 5, she held the cell phone to her ear, afraid to listen, afraid not to.

As Joel's accusations became more crazed, a struggle ensued.

Domestic violence was a familiar evil, and aiding a victim was all in a day's work, but this time, Leilani knew the victim. Carrie's fear had become her own.

As she exited the freeway, she continued to press the phone to her ear, but all she heard was silence.

No more screams, no more shouts.

Still, she prayed for a miracle and continued to Carrie's condominium, heart pounding, adrenaline pumping.

As she neared Carrie's home, she spotted a patrol car in front, red lights flashing and a dispatcher's voice sounding over the radio.

A siren in the distance grew louder. An ambulance? Or more officers on their way?

The window in front of the house had been shattered, the door open wide. She rushed inside, only to find her pregnant friend lying crumpled on the floor, blood seeping into the new beige carpet.

Leilani's heart ached, and her stomach knotted. For a moment, she was afraid she was going to be sick.

"You said you were doing okay," Kay reminded her, drawing her back to the present. "But something tells me you'll carry that horrendous scene with you for a long time."

Leilani took a deep breath, then blew it out. "You're right."

She'd never forget walking into an apartment that had once been cozy and warm, yet in a matter of minutes had been littered with overturned furniture and splattered with blood. Carrie's blood.

Before Leilani could say more or slip back into the memory, the glass of the bay window shattered, and something shot through the kitchen like a missile, striking the stove-top and upsetting a teakettle.

"Oh my God." Leilani jumped to her feet, heart pounding, hands shaking. Accidents happened in the blink of an eye, the beat of a heart, and a loved one could be lost instantly.

Danny.

Where was her son?

Chapter Five

"Danny!"

Maternal worry clogged Leilani's voice, as she turned to face the broken window caused by a flying football, then peered into the backyard, her eyes wide.

"Uh-oh," Danny said. "I'm in big trouble now."

"No you aren't," Luke said. "That was my fault. My throwing arm is a little rusty."

"Yeah, well, it wasn't a bad pass and I missed it. I like football, but don't get to play much. Only at school. And I'm not so good at catching."

Harry chuckled. "Don't worry about it, you two. We've had three boys of our own, not to mention a legion of others. Kay and I are used to mishaps. In fact, we have the phone number of Bayside Glass and Window on speed dial."

That's what Luke liked about Harry. He was always supportive of the guys who'd screwed up yet felt remorseful about it.

Luke placed a hand on his son's shoulder. "Danny and I will have that glass cleaned up and the window repaired before nightfall."

"Well, I'm still super sorry," Danny said. "And I've got money to pay for it."

Luke wasn't going to let that happen, even though instinct suggested he should commend the boy's sense of responsibility.

"I'm picking up the cost of a new window," Luke told Danny. "But I'll let you treat me to an ice cream later today."

"Okay. It's a deal."

Leilani slid open the screen door and stepped out on the porch. The wild-eyed expression she'd worn when she first gaped out the window had subsided a bit. "What happened?"

Danny faced his mother, but he shuffled his feet. "I'm really sorry."

"It wasn't his fault," Luke said, taking the rap for his son. "It was mine. I threw him a bad pass."

Leilani placed trembling hands on her hips. "Then maybe you both ought to come help me clean up the mess in the kitchen."

"Please don't worry about the broken glass," Kay said. "We're used to this sort of thing happening.

And since the food was either in the oven or the fridge, this is merely a little inconvenience."

As Luke and Danny entered the house and surveyed the damages, the doorbell rang.

Joe and Kristin Davenport were the first to arrive, each holding an infant carrier in hand. Introductions were made, and the mess was momentarily forgotten as Kay and Leilani oohed and aahed over the identical twins—girls, born six weeks before.

"Hey, how's it going?" Luke asked Joe, as the two friends shook hands.

"We're not getting much sleep," the firefighter replied. "But we couldn't be happier."

"Where's Bobby?" Luke asked. Joe's son was nearly Danny's age, and he'd hoped the two could meet.

"He's at summer camp this week," Joe said. "Justin, Brett Tanner's son, went, too."

"That's great." The two boys had met about six months before and had really hit it off.

"Kristin and I are going to pick him up on Sunday morning. He's having a blast, but we really miss him."

"I'll bet." Luke nodded toward the baby girls. "I imagine you can always use an extra pair of hands."

"That, too," Joe said. "But Bobby's a neat kid. He and I have gotten really close, and it's not the same at home without him."

Nearly two years ago, Joe had found himself in a situation similar to Luke's. After not seeing Kristin, his high school sweetheart, for years, he ran into her again when she returned to Bayside. And that's when he learned they'd conceived a child he hadn't known about—Bobby.

Luke wanted to talk to him, to share his own news. To ask questions and get some advice. That sort of thing.

But now wasn't the time.

Before Luke could set up some time for the two of them to get together, maybe play a little golf or just meet for a beer, Nick and Hailey Granger arrived with their son in tow.

"Popoo," the dark-haired toddler cried as he dashed toward Harry.

Little Harry Logan Granger hadn't been the first child named after the retired detective, but he was the first to be related by blood.

"Looks like my hands are full keeping this little guy away from the broken glass," Harry said, the chubby-cheeked toddler in his arms. "You'll have to clean up without my help."

"No problem." Luke placed his hand on Danny's shoulder. "We'll have the kitchen back to order in no time at all."

Kay returned from the garage with a broom and a dustpan, and before the breakfast casserole was pulled from the oven, they had the glass picked up and a guy on the way to replace the window.

Leilani's expression, as well as her wan complexion, had gone back to normal—thank goodness—so Luke figured the mishap was behind them.

Throughout the course of the meal—a baked egg-and-potato dish, sliced ham, fresh fruit and an array of muffins—Luke and Leilani shared glances.

He'd never brought a guest to one of Harry's get-togethers before, had never wanted to. But having Leilani and Danny with him made him feel even more a part of something. A family of sorts.

It was a brand-new feeling for Luke, a *good* feeling.

As everyone carried their dishes into the house, making the cleanup easier, a couple of the guys began tossing the football back and forth.

"You better be careful," Danny told them.

"No need to." Joe grinned and sent a spiral to Nick. "The window's already broken."

The men laughed, then as Brett Tanner, a Navy helicopter pilot, and Zack Henderson, a bulldozer operator, joined in, the play became competitive. Brett threw a pass to Zack, and Joe leaped to block it. Both men hit the lawn. Hard.

"Hey," Nick said to Luke. "You and Danny can be on my team."

"Can I, Mom?" Danny gazed at his mother with puppy dog eyes. "Please?"

"No," Leilani said. "Let the men play. You can watch."

"It's no fun to watch," Nick said. "And don't worry, we'll take it easy with him."

"Thanks for asking," she said, "but not today."

Luke opened his mouth to object, but figured it might not be a good idea to get on Leilani's bad side.

Not yet, anyway. He didn't want to put any strain on their relationship while it was so tenuous.

"She always says no," Danny complained in a whisper. "She *hates* football and won't let me do anything fun."

Something told Luke there might be more truth to the boy's statement than the usual exaggerated complaints that kids sometimes made.

Kami had been sheltered his entire life, which Luke had always believed had been a contributing factor in his death. And it looked as though Leilani was bringing up Danny much the same way that she and Kami had been raised.

Luke could understand why she'd want to protect him. She'd lost her mother and father, then her only brother. He suspected she was afraid of losing Danny, too. But an attitude like that wasn't going to do their son any good.

He stole a glance at Leilani, watched her place a gentle hand on Danny's head in a loving caress. He'd need to convince her to cut the kid some slack, but something told him he'd have his work cut out for him.

Especially since Leilani and her family still held Luke responsible for Kami's death.

After Luke paid the glass company for the window repair, he and Leilani thanked the Logans and said their goodbyes.

Once outside the house, they stood curbside, ready to climb into their cars and go their separate ways.

"Thanks for inviting us," Leilani said to Luke. "You were right. The Logans are wonderful people. And I enjoyed meeting everyone else, too."

"I knew you would. For what it's worth, I consider those guys my family."

She nodded, as if she understood his need to connect. As a social worker, she probably did.

Either way, he wasn't ready for the day to end. And the only way he could drag it out was to call in a marker.

"You know, I'm ready for an ice-cream cone," he said to his son. "How about you?"

"We just ate," Leilani reminded them both. "I'm sure Danny doesn't have room for dessert."

"Yes, I do, Mom. I didn't eat any of that egg stuff. Besides, I owe Luke an ice cream. He paid the man for fixing the window, and that's my share." He tossed his mother a crooked grin. "And a deal's a deal, right?"

Leilani crossed her arms, cocking her head slightly as though she might bend on the subject. Obviously Luke wasn't the only one to make that assessment.

"Come on," Danny pleaded. "Please? Otherwise I just have to go watch TV at Aunt Addie's house."

She glanced at Luke, softening even more. "All right. For a little while."

"Want to leave your car here?" he asked.

"No. I'll follow you."

Again, he felt somewhat thwarted. But what the hell—at least she'd agreed to spend more time with him. So he let it go. "There's a great new place in

Bayside Park. It's near that shop where they make fudge in a big copper kettle in the front window. Remember?"

They'd stood outside the place a couple of times, holding hands and breathing in the delicious, chocolaty aroma. At the time, he'd almost been able to believe that life was sweet and that dreams really did come true.

"I know where that is," she said. "I'll follow you there." Then she got into her car.

As Luke unlocked the door of his Expedition, he was reminded that he'd always felt like this with her—on the outside looking in. In fact, he still felt like that a lot of the time. And not just with her.

Even as a kid, he'd never really fit into his own family.

His dad, a college professor, ran off with a graduate student when Luke was ten, leaving his mom, a woman prone to depression, to deal with rejection.

Luke loved his mom, but her depression had been hard for him to deal with as a kid, and he found it easier to avoid being home whenever he could. Even now, his apartment was just a place to sleep or to be alone.

He glanced into the rearview mirror, checking to see if Leilani was still following behind him.

She was.

As he pulled into a parking space in front of Freddy's Frozen Concoctions, one of a string of cutesy shops by the bay that attracted locals and tourists alike, she took the spot next to his.

He tore his gaze from her before she realized he'd been staring and glanced into the back seat, where

Danny sat. The boy waved, and a grin slid across his face, displaying those familiar dimples again.

Would Danny smile like that when Leilani told him his father hadn't died? That he was very much alive and wanted to have a relationship with him?

Luke hoped so.

A boy needed a dad.

And Luke, more than anyone, could attest to that. *He* sure could have used some paternal guidance.

By the time he hit the teen years, he and his mom moved to a run-down apartment in the inner city. With no one to encourage him or keep him in line, he began hanging out with the wrong crowd, drinking, smoking and fighting.

Then he met Leilani, a pretty, college-bound senior who'd recently moved to San Diego. Her smile and the sweet tone of her voice were all it took to grab the rebel inside of him by the scruff of the neck and give him a solid shake.

As he watched Leilani tuck a strand of hair behind her ear, he realized she still had that same effect on him and his endocrine system.

Luke had always found her hula-girl loveliness attractive and arousing. Yet, it had been her innocence and sweet nature that had been the final blow, slamming him with a full-blown crush.

Okay. So his feelings for her had been more serious than that.

He hadn't said the words to her or even admitted them to himself. But he'd never felt anything similar, not before and not after. Looking back, he realized he'd actually loved her.

Of course, she was no longer the same sweet, innocent girl she'd once been. She'd seen the dark and ugly side of life, first with Kami's death, then with her chosen career.

Yet, if truth be told, she still bore that aura of purity—that halo of goodness that mocked all Luke had ever been, all he might ever be. And even with a couple of years maturity and a medical degree under his belt, he still had to try his damnedest not to stare at her like a lovesick puppy.

As she slipped out of the driver's seat, Luke caught a glimpse of her upper leg—tan and still just as shapely as he remembered. When she flashed him a smile, his hormones reacted.

"Is that the place?" Danny pointed to the ice cream shop, which boasted pink-and-white checkered café-style window coverings and a sign that spelled out Freddy's Frozen Concoctions in funky, pastel-colored letters.

"Yes," Luke said. "That's it."

"Can I run ahead and check it out?" he asked.

Leilani paused a moment, as though struggling with the idea of letting him out of sight. But after scanning the area, not more than a fifty-foot radius, she agreed, and he dashed off.

"He's a good boy," Luke said. "You've done a nice job with him."

"Thank you."

As they walked side by side, he caught a faint whiff of her floral fragrance, compelling him to reach for her hand, to claim her as if the years hadn't separated them.

As if Kami hadn't died.

Instead, Luke shoved his hands in the pockets of his slacks, forcing himself to toe the mark.

As a teenager, his "bad boy" reputation had made Leilani uneasy. So, for her sake, he'd done his best to turn over a new leaf. He'd been completely smitten with her back then and even though she'd been shy and reserved, he'd suspected that she'd fallen for him, too.

As summer progressed, so did their relationship. She had him carrying her books, opening doors and brushing up on manners he'd never felt the need for, which he'd grumbled about but secretly hadn't minded. And she'd also secured his promise to quit drinking and carousing for good.

But then Kami had died, and everything they'd felt for each other had died, too.

Well, on her part anyway.

Walking beside her now, he wasn't so sure he'd ever gotten over her. And he had no idea what to do about it.

Inside Freddy's Frozen Concoctions, they joined their son, who was excited about ordering a double scoop of Jelly Bean Surprise, which was loaded with colorful chunks of chewy candy.

Luke ordered a Rocky Road, and Leilani stuck to her earlier decision to pass on ice cream completely.

"Unlike Danny," Leilani said, "I ate plenty of that wonderful egg casserole. So I'll be stuffed until dinner."

"That'll be four dollars and twenty-four cents," the kid behind the counter said.

Leilani reached for her purse, and Luke placed a hand on her arm to stop her. "I can't let you pay unless you get the money from Danny later. He owes me this cone."

The touch, as brief as it was, seemed to surprise them both, as their gazes locked and memories swirled around them.

Sexual awareness and the staggering attraction that had once plagued him, struck his chest like a defibrillator, making it hard to breathe, to speak or to pretend as though nothing had happened.

Common sense told him to release her arm before she jerked away and admonished him for getting too personal, but he couldn't quite bring himself to do so. Not when it had been so long since he'd touched her.

Or since she'd looked at him that way—her eyes a window to her heart, telling him he'd reached something inside of her and taken her breath away.

Luke's touch had shot a jolt of heat through Leilani's bloodstream, and she struggled to find her voice. But the intimate contact had rattled more than her senses. It had also triggered her memories, this time setting off the nice ones. Young love. Shy smiles.

He was right, though. Danny needed to assume

some of the responsibility for the broken window, although she wasn't sure an ice-cream cone and extending their time together was such a good idea.

Nor was she sure that it wasn't.

If Luke was going to be a part of Danny's life, they were going to have to get to know each other—whether she was ready for it or not.

"Of course," she finally said. "The agreement is more than fair. It took two of you to break that window."

Luke grinned, as though they'd reached some parental landmark.

"I'll pay for the cones," she added. "Then, when we get home, Danny will have to get into the cigar box he keeps in his drawer and take it from his savings."

"That works for me." Luke scanned the small shop, noting which tables were already taken, which were available. "It's a nice day. Why don't we take a walk while we eat?"

Leilani knew she ought to decline, to call it a day. But for some reason she let Luke lead them along the concrete walkway that wrapped around the bay, then onto the lawn that edged the sandy shoreline.

Like it or not, Luke was Danny's father. And when the truth came out, he was going to want to spend time with his son. So maybe it wasn't such a bad idea to see what kind of man Luke had become, to get an idea of what kind of father he would be.

If the window incident was any clue, he would play with his son. And if something went wrong, he'd support him. But he would also encourage

Danny to take responsibility for his actions. She couldn't fault him for that.

When they reached the end of the sidewalk, they stood near the edge of the grass and surveyed the vast Pacific.

"This is the end of the line," Leilani said.

"No it isn't," Luke countered. "How long has it been since you walked on the beach?"

Twelve years. At least, that's how long it had been since she walked on this particular stretch of the shore.

"It's been awhile," she admitted. "But we're wearing shoes, and they'll get full of sand."

"There's a way around that." Luke removed his loafers, then his socks, leaving them in the shade of a small sapling.

Danny quickly followed suit.

Leilani had been too busy, too caught up in work and Danny's music lessons to spend time at the ocean. To be honest, she missed the lull of the waves, the call of the gulls, the scent of salt in the air, the feel of wet sand between her toes. So she peeled away the straps of her sandals and bared her feet.

Leaving three pairs of shoes on the grass, they trudged through the dry sand toward the water. Their destination, it seemed, was just as uncertain as their future.

Danny jogged ahead, occasionally leaping over an incoming wave. Along the way, he found a stick and had a sword fight with an imaginary pirate, then chucked it back into the water. He also picked up smaller objects he found in the sand—stones and shells, she suspected. When he found an abandoned red plastic bucket, he immediately put it to use.

Each time he picked up something that he found particularly intriguing or valuable, like the sand dollar he'd just snagged near a clump of seaweed, he would hold his prize up to them and smile, then place it carefully in his bucket.

Luke and Leilani continued to stroll side by side, wrapped up in their own thoughts. Once or twice, their arms brushed against each other, yet they remained silent.

They'd come to the beach a lot when they were dating. And she had to admit that it was those memories, the sweet ones, hovering over her now. Heart flutters, stolen kisses.

As they came upon a hollowed-out wall in the cliff, where erosion had left an artistic swatch of colors and textures, Leilani remembered the familiar spot. They often used to stop there, put down a blanket and watch the sun go down. And on the Fourth of July, they'd watched the fireworks before setting off a few of their own.

It was also the place where they'd made love.

Did Luke remember? She glanced up, caught his eye. In that moment, she knew.

He remembered it just as clearly as she did.

Had he brought her here on purpose? Or had it been an accident, an incident he'd forgotten until something—a glance, a touch, a sea-breezy whisper—triggered the memory?

If she closed her eyes and tried to remember the boy rather than the man, she could almost be that same girl again. That girl, who'd had reservations about a high school romance, especially when her plans called for college in a town nearly three hours away. But their desire for each other had brewed too strong to ignore.

On the night before she was to leave for a college tour, she'd given herself to him. Fully, completely.

He'd been sexually experienced, and she'd been a virgin. But he'd been so gentle, so considerate, so sweet, she could have sworn it had been his very first time, too.

The breeze whipped a strand of hair across her face, but before she could brush it aside, Luke did it for her. His hand lingered near her jaw, then he brushed his knuckles against her cheek, warming her skin. Stirring memories and sensations long forgotten.

The years seemed to peel away, and for a moment, they were two teenagers tiptoeing around their feelings again.

She should step back, laugh it all off. But she couldn't. Not while her heart was pounding, her blood rushing. Her senses whirling.

"I loved you back then," Luke said. "I never told you. But I did. Danny may have been unplanned, but he was conceived in love."

Her mouth opened slightly to form some kind of

a response. At least, that's what she told herself was happening. But as he lowered his head, his lips closing in on hers, the young woman she'd once been stepped forward and placed her hands on his chest. Her fingertips felt the heat of his body, the steady beat of his heart.

She supposed she could push him away, but she could just as easily grab his shirt and draw him closer. Or slip her arms around his neck.

As it was, she stood—helpless against her curiosity and desire—as he brushed his lips across hers. Once. Twice. Soft and sweet.

The kiss began as innocently as their relationship had once been, with the whisper of heat, followed by a surge of fire. As it deepened—as mouths opened and tongues sought to mate—passion, as strong as it had ever been, flared.

This was crazy. Foolish. Just as their relationship had always been.

But Leilani didn't care. Not now. Not while her mind was swirling and her hormones were pumping like there'd been only days separating them instead of years.

She should stop the sweet assault, but she couldn't bring herself to do it. Not yet.

Not until the sound of their son's voice tore through the sea breeze and chased the memories away.

"Hey," Danny hollered as he approached. "What are you guys doing?"

Even if Leilani had wanted to provide her son

with an answer, she couldn't. Not when she didn't have a clue why she'd let that happen.

Or where it was going to lead.

Chapter Six

"What's the deal?"

Danny stood beside them, one hand on his hip, the red sand bucket dangling from the other. He'd obviously come to the conclusion that Leilani hadn't been exactly truthful when she'd downplayed any romantic aspect to her relationship with Luke—past or present.

When the boy didn't receive an answer as quickly as he wanted, he clucked his tongue. "You said you were friends who went to the same school. But it looks to me like you used to be lovebirds."

Leilani felt as vulnerable as one of two little birdies sitting in a tree, K-I-S-S-I-N-G. She cleared her throat. "Yes, well sort of. Luke and I used to date when we were teenagers."

"Was that before you met my dad?" Danny asked.

"Not exactly."

A lie would come so easy right now, as it always had when Danny quizzed her about his father. She'd never meant to deceive him. But the first lie she'd told to her family had set the stage, and one falsehood had built upon another until "Daniel Smith" was a full-blown fantasy man.

She cleared her throat, then stole a glance at Luke, hoping he had some kind of magic response that would make this easy for her, yet knowing there wasn't one. Not if she valued honesty as much as she'd told her son that she did.

Although she would have liked to skirt the issue or postpone the discussion until she and Danny were alone, it was time to untangle the web she'd been weaving for years.

When she looked into her eleven-year-old son's eyes, which were so much like his father's, a multitude of questions lingered there. And so did a budding maturity she hadn't recognized this morning.

"I don't get it," he said. "What does 'not exactly' mean?"

"Luke and I were boyfriend and girlfriend years ago," she began, tap-dancing around the truth and the lie she'd told him.

"Yeah, but what about my dad?" he asked. "Did you go to school with him, too?"

Leilani wanted to dig a hole in the sand and slide all the way to Hong Kong. Instead, she placed a hand on his shoulder. "Let's sit down. I have something to tell you, and it's going to take some time."

The boy crossed his arms, glancing first at Luke, then at his mother. With suspicions and skepticism splashed across his face, and his weight shifted to one leg, he resembled his father more now than he ever had before.

Still, he complied, joining her and sitting on the sand, knees bent and legs crossed.

Luke, however, remained on his feet, distancing himself from the unfolding conversation, yet still an ever-present witness.

"So, what'd you do?" Danny asked. "Cheat on my dad or something?"

"No. I…" Leilani struggled to find the best words, not only to make things right, but to explain on a level a child could understand.

Danny was only eleven, and she'd tried hard to monitor the television shows he watched, the movies she took him to. Yet he seemed to have a handle on some adult concepts.

Where had he picked up on the cheating stuff?

She looked at Luke and saw that he wasn't going to be much help. "Maybe you ought to sit down, too," she told the father of her son.

The old Luke might have shrugged off her suggestion or come up with a snappy retort. But not this Luke. He took a seat next to Danny, then studied the horizon, allowing Leilani to flounder on her own.

For a moment, resentment sparked, but she shook

it off. After all, she'd been the one to create this mess and she would have to fix it. She just hoped Danny would forgive her easily and that there wouldn't be any lasting repercussions on their relationship.

"When you were a little boy," she began, "I wasn't truthful about something."

"You mean you lied?"

It sounded so bad when Danny said it. So wrong. So unforgivable.

She'd had a hundred reasons to lie at the time, but none of them seemed very good right now. "Remember when I told you how sad it was when my little brother died?"

Danny nodded. "Yeah."

Unable to avoid it, she glanced at Luke, saw him staring out to sea, his brow furrowed. She wasn't going to bring up the details of Kami's death or point fingers, if that's what he was afraid of. But her grief had been a contributing factor to their breakup, and she just wanted to… *What?* Justify a decision that didn't seem nearly as sound as it had when she'd made it?

"I was young and grieving," she explained. "And I'd moved back to Lanai. I didn't expect to ever see your father again."

"Because he joined the Navy?" Danny asked.

"No. He wasn't in the military at all. That's the part I lied about."

"How come?" Danny's face contorted in confusion and disappointment.

"At the time I had reason to believe your father

didn't want children, and so I lied to protect you from thinking he didn't want you."

Danny's expression was unreadable, as he stared at the sand for a while. She didn't prod him for a response. She just watched as he piled a small mound in front of him, then stuck a piece of dried seaweed on top like the candle on a make-believe birthday cake.

When he glanced up, as sober as a judge with a gavel in hand, his eyes snagged hers, setting off ripples of remorse and regret through her heart. "You told me he was a hero. And that all the other guys in his unit looked up to him."

"I wanted you to be proud of him."

"You mean he wasn't a SEAL and didn't rescue anyone or save their lives?"

"No." But she hadn't sat down one day and concocted a complicated yarn with the intention of creating a fictional father. She'd merely answered one question after another until the dream dad had evolved into epic proportions.

Her gaze drifted to Luke, and she wondered if he knew she was ready to lay it all on the line—the lie, the truth. She hoped when she did that he wouldn't let Danny down, that he'd truly step up to the plate and be the kind of father a son could really look up to. That he'd take the baton she was handing him and run with it.

"And his name isn't Daniel Smith, either," she admitted.

Luke looked up and caught Leilani watching him,

realizing she was going to go all the way with the revelation. That she was opening up the discussion to him.

He just hoped he didn't blow it. He didn't have a very good bedside manner, which some of the staff members and more than a few patients could attest to. But he would give this conversation his best shot.

"Your father's name is Luke Wynter," he told the boy. "And even though he's not a war hero, the people he works with look up to him. He's also saved a few lives."

Danny scooted around so that he was facing Luke, his eyes zeroing in on him. "*You?* You're my dad?"

Luke nodded.

The boy merely stared at him, and damned if Luke knew how to handle the shocked silence, the frown, the obvious disappointment. Surely he ought to respond, to say something that would make the kid feel better.

But what?

Being a father and saying the right thing to a child was all new to Luke. Hell, his own father had been missing in action most of the time. And the emotional crap Luke had dealt with as a kid, the feelings of abandonment and rejection, had really sucked.

There'd been times when Luke could have used a hand on the shoulder or a "do it for the Gipper" speech. Instead, his old man had left home, walking out when Luke had needed him most.

Thank God Harry Logan had stepped in when he had or Luke might not have recognized the hole in his life. He might never have connected with another male, a man he could look up to and at least try to emulate.

So, as awkward as it felt to take on a paternal role himself, he couldn't just stand by and let his son suffer the same emotional fate. He placed a hand on Danny's shoulder, hoping it was paternal, and caught the boy's eye. "Your mom meant well, but she made an assumption that was wrong."

Danny shot him a skeptical glance, one undoubtedly filled with a few of the same feelings Luke had battled when he'd been the same age, things he didn't want to see his own son wallow in. Or rebel against.

Of course, there was a downside, too. For the first eleven years of his life, Danny had believed in a mythical father, a superhero that a mortal man might never be able to live up to.

A feeling of inadequacy, which was both foreign and unsettling, hovered over Luke. In the past, when faced with emotional discomfort, his natural response had been to say "to hell with it" and withdraw, a defensive ploy that had always worked well.

But no way in hell would he do that to his son.

"Listen, Danny." Luke got up on one knee and leaned toward the boy. "I want to be your dad more than anything in this world."

Their gazes locked. After what seemed like an eternity, Danny shrugged. "I guess I'd like that, too."

A splash of relief washed over Luke. He was veering into uncharted emotional territory, but still, he reached out his hand, hoping to strike up a connection, as well as a bargain.

As their palms touched and they shook, Luke knew his life would never be the same again. And even though he had no clue what to expect in the future, he had to admit that having a son, a family, wasn't nearly as daunting as he'd once thought it might be.

As Luke helped the boy to his feet, Danny turned to his mom, who remained in the sand, sitting primly in her pale yellow sundress, eyes glistening with unshed tears. "You told me to always tell the truth, Mom."

Pain and guilt shot across Leilani's face, and Luke felt compelled to help, to make it easier on her, just as he'd wanted to do after Kami had died.

Would she let him this time?

He wasn't sure.

"I'm sorry," she told Danny. "More than you'll ever know. And I meant every word I ever told you about honesty."

"Yeah," the boy said. "But a lie is still a lie."

"Don't be too hard on her about that," Luke said. "She had reason to believe I wouldn't make a good father back then, but that's not the case. Maybe it was then, but not anymore."

The ring of Luke's cell phone cut through the ocean air. He wanted to ignore the interruption, to continue reinforcing the bond he and Danny had forged, but he was on call again this weekend. And when he recognized Oceana General's number, he had to answer, leaving Leilani and Danny alone in tense silence.

Luke flipped open his cell. "Yes. What is it?"

It was Marge. "I'm sorry to bother you, Luke, but we need you stat."

"What's up?"

"There was a pileup on Interstate 5, and we've got nine accident victims en route. We're short-staffed, so if you can possibly get here…"

"I can." Luke got to his feet. "It's going to take me a while, but I'll be there as quickly as I can."

When he disconnected the line, he turned to Leilani. "That was the hospital. I've got to go."

"Is it Carrie?" she asked, her voice and expression laden with concern.

"No. As far as I know she and the baby are still stable."

"Do you have to go and operate on someone?" Danny asked. "Is that what you do at work?"

"I've had to do that in the past," Luke said, "when a surgeon wasn't immediately available."

"Did the guy you operated on live?" the boy asked, hope glimmering in his eyes as though that might make his old man as heroic as a Navy SEAL.

Luke didn't like to talk E.R. shop or to blow his own horn, but he wanted Danny to think of his *real* father as a hero, to retain part of the "fantasy dad" image. "I saved a few people who would have died if I hadn't stepped in."

"Cool."

"Come on," Luke said. "I've got to get to my car."

As they trudged through the sand, trying to move

as quickly as they could, Luke sensed the tension simmering between mother and son. He wondered if Leilani was going to address it in the car, when they were alone, or whether she was too ashamed to press the boy so soon.

Either way, he figured she was wise in keeping silent for a while. It didn't look as though Danny was going to let her off easy. If he was anything like Luke, he would need some time to come to grips with the truth and to realize his mom hadn't meant to hurt him.

"I'm not sure when I'll be free again today," Luke said, broaching the silence and hoping to help things along. "But how about a trip to Burger Bob's late tomorrow afternoon?"

"Sure," Danny said.

Leilani didn't say anything one way or the other, so Luke assumed the plan met with her approval. If it had just been the two of them, he would have suggested a nicer setting. Maybe Dicarlo's Steakhouse, which was located on the top floor of the Bayside Inn and overlooked the water. But with the romantic ambiance, five-star service and impressive view, DiCarlo's wasn't the kind of place to take a child.

Luke stole a glance at Leilani, trying to gain some insight about what she was thinking, what she was feeling.

A part of him would like to start over and see if they could put the past behind them, maybe take up where they left off. But that would be incredibly naive after all these years.

Still, the old feelings were still there. The heat and chemistry. And that kiss they'd shared proved it.

He suspected a romantic relationship could develop again between them—if they *both* wanted one. But after a twelve-year separation, the most he could hope for was to be on friendly terms with her.

For their son's sake.

After Luke had backed his SUV out of the parking stall and headed to the hospital, Leilani drove Danny to her aunt's house. He sat in the back seat, as he always did for safety reasons, yet she felt more separated from him than ever before.

Still, she'd been moved by Luke's considerate response to Danny, as well as her son's acceptance of the man he'd just learned was his father.

But her deceit—however well-intended—had caused a breach in her relationship with Danny. And although it was still to be seen just how much damage had been done, the silence that filled the car tugged at her heart and knotted her stomach.

"How are you doing?" she finally asked.

"Okay. I still don't get it, though. Luke is pretty cool. Why couldn't you tell me the truth about him?"

She didn't want to go into the intricate and ugly details of Kami's death, nor did she want to explain that Luke had once been a troublemaker who'd skated around delinquency.

"Believe me, Danny. I wish I had told you the truth from day one. And it was a big mistake on my part. I hope you'll learn a lesson from this, too."

As she turned onto Interstate 5 and headed south, he seemed to chew on that until she was ready to exit.

"So how come you and my dad never got married?" he asked.

She'd made up her mind to be honest from here on out, but Danny's age and innocence made that tough, so she struggled to find an answer that would satisfy him, as well as her conscience.

Undaunted by her silence, he continued his interrogation. "Didn't you love him?"

Now that question was easier to answer. "Yes. I did love him."

In spite of their differences.

They'd been raised miles apart, not just in physical distance, but culturally and morally speaking, too. Yet there'd been something about the rebellious teen that had drawn her to him from the very first time she'd spotted him staring at her in English lit. When he'd sauntered toward her after class, tossed her a crooked grin and introduced himself, her interest in him had only grown.

Luke might not have been blessed with a stable and loving home like she'd been, but she'd seen promise in him and had tried to help him turn his life around.

Of course, Aunt Addie hadn't liked the idea one bit. Luke had already established a reputation in the neighborhood. And knowing that he'd had more than a few tussles with the law, Addie hadn't approved of a friendship between the two, let alone a romance.

Stay away from that young thug, she'd said. *He's a bad seed. Don't let him distract you from your studies and lead you astray.*

Leilani, of course, denied her feelings for Luke, even though they'd been growing steadily, and tried her best not to let her grades drop.

She'd told herself he was off-limits in a romantic sense, especially since he'd made it clear he wasn't family-oriented and never wanted to bring children into the world, but that didn't seem to sway her hormones or her desire to see him whenever she had the chance.

They didn't hang out at the usual teen haunts, like the malls, the movie theater or the skateboard park. Instead she'd suggested places like the library or the museums in Balboa Park. And Luke, who'd made her feel like the only girl in the world, had been a completely different guy when he was with her and away from his friends.

He'd been sweet. Considerate. Polite. And he'd made her laugh. He'd also been too darn attractive for words.

After a while, it had been impossible to deny the sparks and the chemistry between them. And one summer night, at their special place on the beach, she succumbed to temptation and gave herself to him.

Luke had been a sensitive lover, and making love, while a bit painful at first, had been an incredible experience. But afterward, for some inexplicable reason, a hodgepodge of emotion had clogged her throat and sent the tears streaming down her cheeks.

"Aw, baby," he'd said. "What's wrong?"

She hadn't been able to tell him. Not when she hadn't been entirely sure herself.

For one thing, the love she'd felt for him at that very moment had been nearly overwhelming, especially since she was going to leave for college soon and had no idea how that would affect them as a couple.

But even though what they'd shared had felt so right, so special, she'd also been slammed by guilt.

Her grandparents had taught her that sex outside of marriage was a sin, and she'd felt as though she'd somehow let them down.

When Luke had dropped her off at the house, Aunt Addie had suspected they'd been together, and fearing that the woman would be able to figure out what they'd done, Leilani had denied being with Luke. She'd claimed to have been with a couple of girlfriends and to have run out of gas on the interstate.

Guilt had snaked around her like a python, making it tough to breathe and marring what she and Luke had shared, what they'd felt. The following day, she'd gone to Los Angeles for a welcome-weekend at the college she would attend in a few short weeks. The next night, she'd gotten word that Kami had been killed and that she needed to come home immediately.

Regret had compounded her guilt and made her

feel just as much to blame for her brother's tragic death as Luke had been. Just as reckless.

And now, years later, she would have to face Aunt Addie and admit that she'd not only lied back then, but she'd perpetuated the fallacy over time.

To say she dreaded that confrontation was an understatement. Disappointing her aunt might, in some ways, be more difficult than telling Danny had been, more damaging to the family dynamics.

As she turned into the driveway that led to the gated, underground parking lot of Eberly Arms, she glanced into the rearview mirror at her son. "Let's not tell Aunt Addie about Luke just yet. Okay?"

"Why not?"

What was she supposed to tell him? That Luke had taken Kami to a wild party that had been inappropriate for either of them to attend? That, while under the influence of drugs, her sweet fourteen-year-old brother, an honor student, had been killed?

That her family hadn't forgiven Luke yet?

That she hadn't, either?

No, she couldn't bring herself to admit all of that to her son. Not now. And maybe not ever.

Instead, she said, "Because I told that lie about your father to everyone. And I need to be the one to explain it to Aunt Addie, to tell her I'm sorry. To face the consequences of her disappointment and to make things right."

The mind was a funny thing, wasn't it?

It could rationalize any decision, she supposed.

But in her heart of hearts, there was another reason not to tell Aunt Addie just yet. Once Addie knew the identity of Danny's father, she was going to inject her harsh version of the past into the mix.

Every child deserved a father he or she could look up to, and Leilani wanted no less for her son.

She just hoped that when Addie got wind of the truth, Luke wouldn't topple off the pedestal on which Danny had placed him.

Chapter Seven

The next afternoon, Luke drove to the Eberly Arms apartment complex, where Leilani and Danny stood on the sidewalk, waiting for him.

Leilani, as lovely as usual, wore a pair of black cropped pants and a simple, light blue cotton blouse—nothing fancy or revealing. But she didn't need to dress suggestively to make his blood pump faster—it did each time he laid eyes on her.

To this day, he still found her sexy, something that neither time nor motherhood had altered.

He pulled in alongside the curb, the engine of his Expedition idling, and rolled down the passenger window. "I would have come to the door."

"We thought we'd make it easier for you." She

smiled, then climbed into the vehicle, as Danny got in the back seat.

Luke had a sneaking suspicion Leilani hadn't wanted him to knock on her aunt's door, but at least she'd agreed to ride with him.

It was a start, he supposed.

Once they'd closed the doors and secured their seat belts, Luke pulled onto the street and headed toward Burger Bob's, a local hamburger place that, according to what he'd heard, was a favorite of the kids in town.

Leilani, with her glossy black hair curled under at the shoulders, remained quiet. Pensive. Intriguing.

Danny, on the other hand, picked up the slack, chattering about the upcoming baseball play-offs and why the Los Angeles Angels stood a whole lot better chance of making it than the San Diego Padres did.

Joe Davenport, a good friend who'd also been one of the troubled teenagers Harry Logan had mentored, had season tickets on the third baseline at Petco Park. He'd offered them to Luke on several occasions, but Luke had always declined, using his work schedule as an excuse.

He'd make the time now, though. For his son.

Ten minutes later, Luke turned into the parking lot at Burger Bob's.

As Danny got out of the Expedition, he studied the rainbow-colored climbing structure that began inside the family restaurant and extended outside. "Wow. That's cool."

"I thought you'd like it." Luke stole a glance at Leilani, who stood beside him.

"Great choice, Luke. That playground is a child's paradise." Her eyes held a glimmer of excitement he hadn't seen in years, and he struggled not to take her by the hand and pretend that nothing had changed between them.

Instead, they walked side by side, the distance between them more than physical.

As they entered Bob's, Luke placed a hand on his son's upper back. "Do you want to order something to eat now? Or would you rather play?"

Danny shrugged. "Whatever. If you guys need time to talk, I can keep busy."

Luke risked another glance at Leilani.

For a man who commanded immediate response and results in the E.R., he felt like an alien in a family situation. And landing smack-dab in a Burger Bob setting, he felt about twelve rocks from the sun.

"It's completely up to you," Leilani told the boy.

"Well, I kind of want to check out the playground, but I'd also like to hang out with you guys and talk to Luke. Or my dad." Danny scrunched his face. "What am I suppose to call you?"

Luke thought about all the words and phrases he used when referring to his old man, knowing that wasn't what Danny meant. But he figured he couldn't very well waltz into the boy's life and claim a relationship they'd never shared. Besides, a man had to earn the title of Dad. "Why don't you call me Luke until you feel like calling me something else."

"Okay." Danny's gaze drifted to the climbing structure, where two boys about his age had just dashed. "Maybe I'll play."

"Be careful," Leilani said.

"I will."

As Danny scampered off, the awkward parents slid onto the red vinyl seats in a corner booth. Their hands rested on the white Formica tabletop. Luke suspected Leilani wasn't any more comfortable than he was, but there was no getting around the eggshells they were walking on.

"Can I get you something to drink?" he asked.

"Thanks. A diet soda would be nice."

He nodded, suddenly wishing Burger Bob served beverages a lot stronger than soda pop. "Will Danny want a cola?"

"If they have root beer. That's his favorite."

Luke would make a note of that. His son also liked baseball and was an L.A. Angels fan.

"Then, if you'll excuse me," he said, "I'll place the drink orders."

When he returned, he set a tissue-lined basket of fried zucchini and a small container of ranch dressing on the table in front of her. "Do you still like to eat these?"

She smiled. "I try to stay away from greasy food, but yes, I do."

The fact that he'd remembered seemed to please

her, at least the warm sparkle in her eyes implied that it had, but the old memory of a snack preference certainly hadn't done much to break the conversational ice.

Damn. This was awkward. And she wasn't helping the conversation along, so he was on his own.

"How did it go?" he asked. "I mean, after you took Danny home yesterday."

She shrugged. "All right I suppose. He wasn't happy about being lied to."

Luke wasn't happy about it, either. He wished Leilani would have told him when she'd found out she was pregnant. But then again, he wished they'd both made different choices back then. Too bad they couldn't enter a time warp, wipe the slate clean and start over.

If they could, he'd begin by sticking close to home that Saturday night in July, no matter how badly his friends had been ragging on him to join them.

Hindsight was great, wasn't it? A person could get rich if he were able to bottle and sell it.

"Hey," Danny called out from a section of the bright yellow tunnels suspended overhead, where he'd been crawling. When his parents glanced up, he waved, then took off through the tubes, behind a boy in a red T-shirt.

"He makes friends easily," Leilani said, as she eyed the platter of zucchini.

Luke pushed it toward her. "One little bite won't hurt."

"Are you trying to tempt me?" The start of a smile formed, then stalled.

They'd both faced temptation back then, but he

hoped she didn't think he'd taken on the serpent role. Her innocence and beauty might have taunted him to distraction, but he hadn't been foolish enough to believe a girl like her might fall for a hard-ass rebel like him. He hadn't meant to take advantage of her, no matter how badly he'd wanted to be her lover.

He couldn't help but wonder if time had changed things. Were they on a level playing field now?

Maybe they'd been star-crossed lovers from the get-go. Maybe they'd been destined to crash and burn no matter when they'd met.

Leilani took a deep-fried zucchini strip, dipped it into the creamy white dressing and popped it in her mouth. He watched her eat, a sated expression on her face.

"Mmm. It's really good. I haven't had one of these in a long time." She glanced at Luke, apparently realizing he'd been studying her intently.

Had she picked up on any romantic vibes? Had she sensed that he'd like to start over? Start fresh?

Probably not at a place like this. Not with all the noise and clatter from the kitchen or the kids shrieking as they climbed up red canvas netting, crawled through blue and yellow plastic tunnels overhead or slid down purple tubular slides into a vat of multi-colored plastic balls.

And there was no way he could even broach a subject like that until he apologized and they were able to put the past behind them.

He cleared his throat, then stepped out on a brittle

limb, hoping he wasn't stirring up a subject better left alone. "I want you to know how sorry I am about what happened to Kami."

She paused in mid-chew, half a zucchini in her hand. "I'm sorry, too."

"If I'd had any idea that there had been drugs involved at that party, I wouldn't have let him set foot on the property, let alone go inside."

She merely studied him, her eyes filling with unshed tears. "I think it's best if we try to forget about that night and talk about something else."

Was it? Getting it out in the open would be a good way to lance a wound and promote healing. But then again, maybe this wasn't the time or place.

In a sense, it seemed as though she was telling him that she no longer held the accident against him. But he couldn't help wishing she'd say the words: *It wasn't your fault, Luke.*

Or even if she still thought he was to blame, he wanted to hear: *I forgive you.*

Instead, to change the subject, he reached into his pocket and pulled out a check he'd written earlier. It was for five thousand dollars.

"What's this?" she asked wide-eyed.

"It's just a start on what I owe you for past child support."

"You don't owe me any money. I'm not even sure I want you to give me any from now on. I made a decision to have the baby on my own, fully expecting to support him myself."

"I don't care. That's all in the past." According to her, that was something they were supposed to be putting behind them.

Still, he had a feeling their particular past—as painful and regret-filled as it was—would never be very far out of sight or out of mind.

Moments later, Danny joined them, easing the tension. "When it's time to eat, can I have a kid's meal? Joey, one of the boys I was playing with, said they have these cool morphing monsters packed inside."

"Sure." Luke looked at Leilani. "What do you want?"

"How about a grilled chicken sandwich?"

"You got it." Luke slid from his seat at the booth, then went to place the order.

Before long, he returned with their food.

While they ate, Luke told Danny that he would try and get tickets for a baseball game soon.

"That would be way cool, wouldn't it, Mom?"

"Yes, it would."

The rest of their time together passed easily, with Danny filling Luke in on the things that interested him, the television shows, the games he played, books he read.

Luke would have loved to have extended their time together, but he hated to push, so after they ate, he drove them back to the Eberly Arms.

He pulled up along the same curb where he'd picked them up, close to the spot where two older ladies stood by the wrought iron doors that opened to the garage. One woman, a redhead, who'd apparently been walking two little white dogs on a leash, chatted with the other.

"Hey, there's Aunt Addie and her friend who has the cockatiels," Danny said.

"Cockapoos," Leilani corrected.

"What's the difference?" he asked.

"For one thing," Luke said, "one has feathers and the other has fur."

The silver-haired woman, her hair coiffed like a steel helmet, turned and, spotting Leilani in the front seat of the SUV, smiled warmly. But when her gaze traveled to the driver's seat, her expression froze as recognition turned to contempt.

Luke might still have feelings for Leilani—whatever they were—but he could see now that there wasn't any hope for a relationship to develop between them.

Not until both she and her family forgave him.

And a scowl on Addie Stephens's face suggested that Luke shouldn't expect that to happen in his lifetime.

As Luke drove away, Leilani took one look at her aunt and knew Addie had not only recognized him, but that she hadn't been one bit happy to see the friend with whom Leilani and Danny had spent the afternoon and early evening.

Hopefully, Addie wouldn't discuss her thoughts, feelings or opinions about Luke in front of Danny.

"Hey, Ricky and Lucy." Danny dropped to his knees to greet Eleanor Townsend's beloved dogs.

The cockapoos were every bit as happy to see the boy as he was to see them. "How are you guys?"

"Good evening, ladies," Leilani said.

Addie pressed her lips shut, but a frown implied there was a storm cloud of trouble brewing on the horizon.

On the other hand, the elderly widow, whose flaming-red hair came from a bottle, smiled warmly. "Why, hello, Lani. Addie said you two went out with a friend. But I assumed it was a woman, not a handsome man."

"It's not what you think," Leilani told Mrs. Townsend, hoping Addie would know the words were intended for her, too. "Luke and I went to school together. We hadn't seen or talked to each other in years, then we met again at the hospital the other night. He's a doctor now."

She risked a glance at her aunt, hoping that bit of news would soften the blow.

"You both went to school in Hawaii?" Eleanor Townsend asked.

Leilani wasn't sure how much her aunt had revealed to her friend about the past, but Mrs. Townsend obviously knew that Leilani's father, a Navy corpsman, had been stationed in Honolulu, where he'd met and fallen in love with her mother. And that Leilani had been born and raised in the islands.

After Leilani's parents died, Addie came to Hawaii a couple of times each year to visit. She did, however, finally get her wish.

"I moved to San Diego right before my senior year," Leilani explained. "My family decided it would be best if I moved in with Aunt Addie and attended school here. And that's where I met Luke."

Kit Carson High had been—and still was—a local magnet school that provided a prestigious program with advance placement courses. Leilani's family had hoped that if she excelled there, as she'd always done in her classes, that she would have a better choice of colleges.

"Well, he's gorgeous," Mrs. Townsend said. "And a doctor to boot. Perhaps you two will fall in love, and then you can settle in the area, closer to Addie." Mrs. Townsend grinned like a Cheshire yenta. "Wouldn't that be nice?"

Addie's frown deepened. "You and I can talk about that later, Eleanor."

Mrs. Townsend seemed to pick up on the hint and let the subject drop.

"Danny, don't let those dogs get wound up in their leashes." Leilani hoped addressing the boy would remind her aunt of his presence. Danny didn't need to hear Addie rant about the unfairness and injustice of Kami's death. Or about how Luke had been the cause of a devastating loss for the family who'd had more than its fair share of death already.

And Leilani didn't need to hear it, either. Not when she was trying to put it all behind her for her son's sake.

"Well," Leilani said, wanting to excuse herself.

"I'd better get Danny upstairs and in the shower. It'll be bedtime before we know it."

"Aw, Mom," Danny complained. "Can't I play with Ricky and Lucy a little more?"

Maybe that would be all right. In the past, her aunt had never liked to discuss Kami's death in front of Danny, especially since it had been drug-related.

Leilani scanned the neighborhood, quiet now. "All right. Will you look after Danny, Aunt Addie?"

"Of course. I'm not going to drag him off to any parties."

The words hit their mark, as Leilani turned and punched in the code that would open the wrought iron gate manually and allow her into the complex.

Once Addie had said goodbye to her friend and returned to the apartment, Leilani expected a private confrontation. And sure enough, she'd been right.

Thank goodness it took place after Danny had gone to bed.

"You've always been a good girl," Addie said, as she plopped down on the worn, green plaid sofa. "As a child, you were not only pretty, but compassionate. And bright. You still are. For the life of me, I can't understand your fixation with that boy."

"*That boy* is now a respected doctor," Leilani said, bolstering her own opinion about Luke and the changes he'd made.

"Good for him. Kami might have gone to medical school, too."

The truth of her statement snaked around Leilani, squeezing out another wave of remorse. Of grief.

"What were you doing with him today?" her aunt asked.

"Luke and I used to be good friends, Addie. In fact, we still are." That's as close to the truth as Leilani could get for now.

"Did you forget what he did to Kami?"

"He didn't *do* anything to him. He was negligent. Thoughtless. And he was guilty of making a stupid decision."

"Kami paid the price."

They all had, it seemed.

Leilani's family, to be sure, but Luke had paid a price, too.

And she feared Danny's day was coming.

The next night, as Luke read the lab report on the blood work of an elderly man suffering from severe abdominal pain, he glanced at the clock, wondering what Leilani and Danny were doing right then.

Sleeping, he supposed.

In the past, he hadn't missed having a nine-to-five life, even though his work schedule wasn't conducive to relationships—romantic or otherwise. It hadn't bothered him before. In fact, he'd been happy to have a ready excuse to keep to himself. But his night hours were going to make it difficult to spend quality time with Leilani and Danny.

He scanned the numbers on the report, then diagnosed appendicitis and asked Marge to call in the resident surgeon. All he had to do was notify the patient and his wife of the lab results and what they meant, then it was on to the next case.

That's one reason Luke had chosen to specialize in emergency medicine. He had an innate ability to make quick, sound diagnoses and decide upon the best life-saving treatments. He also loved the excitement, the pace. The rush.

Working in the E.R. also meant he didn't have to get too close to his patients—too attached—which made it much easier on those occasions when a patient didn't pull through.

True to form, Luke went through the motions this evening, explaining his diagnosis to Ralph Gleason and his wife, answering their questions. After telling them that Dr. Wellington would be stopping by to tell them when surgery had been scheduled, he made a couple of notes on the chart. When he finished, he stopped by the nurses' station, where someone had left a plate of brownies for the staff.

Luke had a thing for sweets, especially chocolate, so he reached for one and took a bite. Not bad.

"Doctor, can I get you a cup of coffee?" Elena Rodriguez, an R.N. who just transferred to the E.R. from pediatrics, flashed him a pretty smile.

Luke turned, a frosted brownie in his hand. "No thanks. I've had more than my share already."

"If there's anything you need…"

There wasn't.

A flirtatious glimmer in Elena's pretty brown eyes made him aware of the double meaning behind her offer.

Young, single women often came on strong before they realized Luke didn't usually date anyone on staff at Oceana. This particular twenty-something brunette would figure that out soon enough.

"Thanks, Elena. I'll keep that in mind." But he wouldn't. Even if he changed his mind about dating another woman he worked with, he wouldn't go out with Elena. He was too caught up with Leilani, too determined to mend the invisible fences that separated them.

The rest of the night passed much the same, with periods of crises that caused the hands on the clock to spin and periods of calm, when the staff, who could evolve into a well-oiled machine if necessary, let loose and became human.

During one of the quiet spells, Luke took a break and went to the ICU to check on Carrie. It was becoming a habit, but he wanted to know how she was doing, what changes had taken place, what the current prognosis for her recovery was.

The neurosurgeon and the obstetrician had been keeping him posted, but he wanted an update. Later today, after he'd gotten some sleep, he planned to stop by the ICU visiting room with hopes of seeing Leilani again and answering any questions she might have.

Yeah, right. That's the excuse he gave himself. But the truth was he wanted to be near her. And he wanted to convince her that he was a new man, someone she could respect and look up to.

What was wrong with that?

Once at the doorway he punched in the code, then let himself in and proceeded to the nurses' station, where he was surprised the see Bethany Paige the redhead he'd dated for a short time a few months ago. Bethany had been one of the few who'd caused him to temporarily disregard his reluctance to fish off the hospital pier.

"Fancy meeting you again." Her smile let him know she was pleased to see him.

"How's Ms. Summers doing?" he asked. "Any change from last night?"

"Not really."

He nodded. There was no way of knowing if she'd suffered any brain damage. He suspected there'd be some. "Have her contractions started up again?"

"Not on my shift. But from what I understand, Dr. Ernst, the neonatologist assigned to monitor the baby's condition, believes he may have suffered a hairline fracture of the skull, but there's no apparent bleeding or swelling."

Luke nodded. After such a severe beating, Carrie and the baby were lucky to have survived at all.

"Forgive me for prying, but you've gotten very involved in this case, which is a first for you." Bethany crossed her arms and eyed him carefully. "If I didn't know better, I'd wonder if that baby was yours."

Luke looked up, brows furrowed, and shot her a you've-got-to-be-kidding look.

"But I *do* know better," Bethany said. "You told me that you don't take chances like that because you're not daddy material."

He wasn't.

At least, he hadn't thought he was. But Danny deserved to have a dad who would give fatherhood a try.

"Let me set the record straight and put the kibosh on any potential rumors. That baby isn't mine. And for what it's worth, the first time I laid eyes on his mother was when she was wheeled into the E.R." Then he turned and walked away, back to the E.R.— where he belonged. Back to the patients who moved in and out through a revolving door.

As he made his way down the hall and onto his turf, he spotted Marge striding toward him, the soles of her shoes squeaking on the linoleum. "Dr. Wynter?"

"Yes?"

"The paramedics are bringing in a drug-overdose. She's fifty-two and, according to her daughter, she's been despondent over a recent divorce. ETA is three minutes. We'll be taking her to bed six."

His gut clenched, as it always did when faced with a patient who'd tried to end his or her life, and it knotted all the tighter as he sympathized with the patient's daughter.

The day his mom had ended her life, Luke had been wrapping up his second year at Cabrillo Junior

College and had stopped by her apartment to wash his clothes in the Laundromat at her complex. At first, when he spotted her on the couch with the television set on, he thought she'd dozed off. But an empty pill bottle and an open pint of Scotch suggested otherwise.

She'd been alive when he'd found her, barely. He'd called the paramedics, and they'd responded quickly, but she'd died en route to the hospital.

Lisa Wynter had been battling depression for years, and even though Luke knew—intellectually— that he wasn't to blame, he couldn't help feeling that he'd failed her in some way.

Maybe that's why he'd let Harry talk him into going to med school, so he could prove himself. And in a sense, he had, graduating at the top of his class.

Moments later, the paramedics rolled in the woman who'd ingested an entire bottle of sleeping pills, and Luke let the past go as he slipped into "super doc" mode and dealt with the medical emergency at hand. When her stomach had been pumped and she'd been stabilized, he sent her to ICU for monitoring. Then she'd be taken to the psych ward, where they were better able to deal with her despondency and the other issues that had led to her decision to end it all.

Senseless deaths—the accidents, the murders, the suicides—had a way of wearing on some physicians if they let them.

For the most part, Luke didn't let them.

He thrived in the E.R. setting at Oceana General,
where the night shift kept him too busy to think about
the tragedy that took Kami's life and nearly ruined his
own. Where he was able to take pride in himself for
mending the bodies of people he'd never see again.

And it worked—until they rolled in a stretcher
carrying a bloodied kid or an unconscious woman
who'd tried to do herself in.

Then he had to face the cold hard facts.

Deep inside, there was a part of him that was
still broken.

A part of him that would never heal.

Chapter Eight

As the sun began to rise over Oceana General and Luke's shift was ending, Marge made her way toward him.

"Doctor?"

He glanced up from the chart he was reading. "Yes?"

"We just received a call from the ICU. Carrie Summers's water broke, and they'll be doing an emergency C-section in about an hour."

Luke, whose concern and involvement in Carrie's case had become common knowledge to the ICU staff, had asked to be notified and kept abreast of any changes to her condition.

"Bethany Paige suggested that you might want to be the one to notify Ms. Summers's friend." Marge handed him a slip of paper with Leilani's number, or rather, that of her aunt.

There was a hospital protocol to be followed about notifying the next of kin, and allowing Luke to make that call wasn't exactly policy.

"Tell Bethany that she was right. I'll take care of the notification." Luke put away the chart he'd been studying. "And thank her for me."

Marge nodded, then did as he asked. If she wondered why Carrie's condition had sucked Luke in when so many others hadn't, she didn't question him.

Stealing a private moment, Luke picked up the phone and dialed. It wasn't quite five-thirty, so the ring would probably wake the entire household.

He braced himself to hear Mrs. Stephens answer and to catch the animosity in her tone when she recognized his voice. The older woman had never liked him, even before Kami died, and Luke had no reason to believe that her opinion of him would ever change.

Normally, he didn't give a damn about what people thought, but this case was different. Addie adored Leilani and vice versa, so he'd always tried to be polite and respectful. Still, it hadn't seemed to matter.

He hadn't been able to do a single thing to change her mind in the past, and something told him that ten years of keeping his nose clean and a medical degree wouldn't make a dent in her opinion of him now.

The phone was answered on the second ring, and thankfully it was Leilani's voice that responded with a sleepy "Hello."

"It's me, Luke. Carrie is having a caesarian this morning, and I thought you might want to be here."

"Oh my God. Is she okay? Did something go wrong?"

"As far as I know, her water broke and Dr. Gray has decided to deliver today. They're calling in the neonatalogist and getting things ready now."

"Are the baby's lungs developed? I know they'd given him medication to help with that, but did it work?"

"They believe so." But until the neonatologist could give Carrie's baby a thorough exam, they wouldn't know for sure what damage that beating had done. But no need to go into that with Leilani. Not on the telephone.

"Good." Leilani started to blow out a sigh of relief, then caught herself. "Uh-oh. I just remembered Aunt Addie needs to go to the bank today and has a few other errands to run, so she'll need the car. But maybe she can ask a friend to take her. Or better yet, I'll take a cab."

"If you'll give me time to wrap up a few things here, I'll come by and pick you up. Then I'll wait with you."

When she didn't respond to his offer, he suspected she might be trying to come up with a polite way to tell him to mind his own business. That she didn't need his support. Or him.

"Thanks," she finally said. "That way I won't leave my aunt without a vehicle. And to be honest, I'd like to have someone sit with me."

A goofy sense of relief settled over him. He wasn't

sure why. Maybe because she was going to let him hold her hand through the ordeal—figuratively speaking, of course.

"Are you sure your aunt won't mind watching Danny for you today?" he asked.

"Of course not. She loves him like her own."

"That's good." Too bad Addie thought Danny's father was the lowest form of pond scum. "Then I'll be at your place in about thirty minutes."

"All right. I'll tell my aunt where I'm going, then I'll get ready and be waiting for you out front."

Fortunately, Luke was able to leave the hospital sooner than he expected, and at ten minutes to six, he got to the Eberly Arms complex, just as a small Toyota Corolla pulled out of the underground garage. While the gates slowly closed, he zipped inside. After snagging a parking place near the trash bins, he took the elevator to the fourth floor, strode down the musty hall and knocked lightly on the door.

Fortunately, Leilani answered. "I was going to meet you downstairs."

It was possible that she was in a hurry to get to the hospital, but he suspected she also meant to prevent him from running into her aunt. But he wouldn't stew about it.

"I got away sooner than I expected," he explained.

"Good. I'm ready." She'd dressed casually in a pink, scoop neck T-shirt, a lightweight pair of white sweats and tennis shoes. And even though her hair was still damp from the shower, and it appeared that she'd rushed to throw herself together, she still looked great.

He opened his mouth to tell her so, then clamped it shut. There was no need to get mushy or to fawn over her. It wasn't his style. But then again, being around Leilani had always made him want to be a different man.

A better one.

Yet something told him that in her eyes and in those of her aunt's he'd always fall short, which was too bad. Luke didn't intend to set himself up for failure, which would be inevitable when it came to anything romantic developing between them. He'd learned that the last time.

Some relationships were over before they began.

He nodded toward the navy-blue canvas tote bag she carried in her right hand. "I see you're prepared to stay awhile."

"That first night I sat with Carrie was a bit rough. And not having a toothbrush or anything else I needed wasn't fun. So I packed a few necessities to have handy—just in case." She snatched the purse that rested on the lamp table.

Luke waited until she'd secured the house, then walked her to the elevator, where they waited side by side. He caught a pleasing whiff of milled bath soap, something feminine and nice. The kind sold in specialty shops rather than off a grocery store shelf.

She was as fresh and clean as the morning dew on a sprig of lilacs, which only reminded him that he'd been working all night and that he hadn't shaved or showered since he'd left for the hospital more than ten hours ago.

He hoped he didn't smell rank. He also hoped the handful of breath mints he'd popped into his mouth when he'd left the hospital had chased away the taste of the overbrewed coffee he'd been chugging down throughout his shift.

When the elevator doors opened, they stepped inside, then turned and faced the front, waiting for the numbers to light up and mark their descent. It took all Luke's resolve not to turn his attention to her, to reach out and take her hand in his. To give it a squeeze and tell her everything would be okay, even though he was a realist and knew that in a case like Carrie's, when there were so many unknown variables involved, some things were hard to predict.

Still, he couldn't help bumping his arm against hers, much like he used to do when they'd been dating and he'd wanted to get her attention.

When her gaze caught his, he asked, "Are you all right?"

Leilani nodded. "Yes, I'm fine." And she was. Now that he was here.

In the enclosed quarters of the elevator, a light hint of Luke's cologne, a musky, sea-breezy scent, taunted her, and she had an overwhelming urge to lean toward him, to try and capture another whiff.

"Thanks for calling me," she said instead, watching the numbers over the door light up—

3...2...1...G. "And for offering to take me to the hospital and sit with me."

"No problem."

"I'm a little nervous and worried about what today might bring." She held out her hand, showed him how her fingers trembled a bit. "And I'm usually as cool as a cucumber when I need to be."

"It's a lot easier when you're not personally involved. That's the main reason I chose to specialize in emergency medicine."

Luke was right about it being easier when working with strangers. She wondered if he'd ever had to treat a friend who was injured or sick.

Harry Logan, who'd had open heart surgery a few years ago, and his wife, Kay, who'd had a recent biopsy, came to mind. So she suspected he spoke from experience.

As the doors opened, Leilani took a step, only to have her foot catch on a frayed, loose piece of carpet, causing her to lurch forward.

Luke reacted quickly, grabbing her before she fell flat on her face. "Are you sure you're okay?"

Yes. No.

As their eyes met, something spellbinding swept over her, causing her heart to ricochet through her chest like the silver bearing shooting through a pinball machine. All that thumping and ba-bumping set off a slew of lights and bells and whistles inside.

He helped her straighten, and when she was steady again, he released her. She ought to be grateful to be in control of herself again, yet a strange sense of loss settled over her. She missed the feel of his arms, the strength of his chest, the warmth of his embrace.

As if sensing her need, he reached for her hand, and they walked through the dank garage together, their shoes crunching on the dirty concrete.

"You really are shaky," he said.

"I was only a bit jittery until my toe caught that spot in the carpet. But I'll be okay once my adrenaline quits pumping. I'm just a little worried about Carrie and the baby."

Another man might have told her not to give it a second thought, that everything would be all right. But Luke was a doctor, and she didn't think he would blow smoke just to get her to feel better.

Instead, he drew her to a stop, then turned to face her, cupping her cheek with his free hand. "I can't make promises about the outcome, but I can tell you that Arlene Gray is the best obstetrician around. And that Jim Ernst specializes in high-risk newborns. Carrie and her baby couldn't be in better hands." Luke's words sent a soothing message to the butterflies in her stomach and the nerves in her hands.

"Thanks, Luke. I'll keep that in mind."

And she'd keep a few other things in mind, too. Luke had been more than a friend during this ordeal, and she appreciated his support. She'd always tried to be a source of strength for others, so it was nice to have someone to lean on for a change. It also made her feel much better about Luke taking on a paternal role in Danny's life.

Minutes later, after climbing into his Expedition, they were on their way to Oceana General. To the baby she'd promised to protect.

"You said that Carrie asked you to take care of her son," Luke said.

"That's right."

"Did she give you legal custody?" he asked. "Is it written up in a will or other document?"

"No. At least, I don't think so. There wasn't any time." His question provoked one of her own. "Why do you ask?"

"Because it would help to have a legal guardian making decisions about the baby's health-care, since Carrie isn't able to do it herself."

"A policeman overheard her tell me what she wanted. Does that count?"

"When was that?"

"The night she was beaten." Leilani glanced out the window, at the quiet city streets. "She'd mentioned it earlier in the day, when we met at her house and went out to lunch. Then, that night, after Joel broke into her house and hurt her, she asked me again. In front of a witness."

"I thought she was unconscious."

"She was awake when I arrived."

Leilani's heart had been in her throat when she'd entered the crime scene that had, hours earlier, been a lovely, two-bedroom condo decorated in shades of green and beige. The place was a mess and she'd had to step around overturned furniture—a chair, an end table, a broken lamp—as well as shards of glass from the shattered front window.

A police officer was kneeling beside Carrie, who lay in a bloodied heap on the floor.

Leilani had dropped to her knees at her friend's side and had gently placed a hand on Carrie's shoulder, trying not to cause any additional pain. "I'm here, Carrie. And an ambulance is on the way. Hold on. Everything will be all right." She'd glanced at the police officer, and his gaze met hers. So had his skepticism.

Carrie's eyes flickered. "Lani? Is that you?"

"Yes, it's me."

"The baby." Carrie had grimaced in pain. "Please don't let anything happen to him."

"I won't," Leilani had whispered, realizing she was making a promise she had little power to keep. She'd been afraid the child might not have survived the attack on its mother.

Carrie looked at the officer, her eyes pleading. "If anything…happens…I want Lani to have my baby. To raise him."

The officer nodded, as if the three of them had entered some kind of legal, binding agreement.

Carrie turned to Leilani. "I've been calling him Michael." Then she closed her eyes and slipped into unconsciousness—a condition that still plagued her.

Dear God, Leilani prayed silently. *Please let Carrie come to soon.*

And let her become the mother she's always wanted to be.

Michael Summers was born at 8:16 that morning and weighed in at four pounds, three ounces.

Two other babies, twins who also came into the world via C-section nearly an hour later, had been brought to the regular nursery already. There, while their proud daddy watched, the two newborn girls had their tiny feet printed. Then, after being weighed and measured, they were bathed and swaddled.

Carrie's baby had gone directly to the neonatal intensive care unit. Luke had managed to learn that Dr. Ernst was giving him a thorough exam and that, so far, everything was going well.

"When do you think we can see him?" Leilani asked Luke, who'd stayed with her all morning.

"We should hear something pretty soon."

As the twins were wheeled away, probably to be with their mother in her room, Leilani nudged Luke. "Do you think something went wrong? Or maybe we're supposed to be waiting somewhere else and they can't find us?"

Before Luke could respond, a nurse poked her head out the nursery door. "Dr. Wynter?"

"Yes?"

"You two can come back now."

Luke reached for Leilani's hand and drew her to a stand. Then they walked into the nursery where they were instructed to wash their hands and put on sterile gowns and blue disposable booties over their shoes.

"The neonatal intensive care unit is for the sickest of babies," Luke told Leilani, "and they're very careful about protecting them from outside germs."

"If you're finished dressing, you can follow me." The R.N. led them into a separate room that served as the neonatal intensive care unit. They passed the incubators of several other preemies. It was tough seeing such critically ill newborns, most of whom were on oxygen and connected to monitors. But not all of them appeared to be premature. An apparently full-term infant, whose umbilicus had been freshly cut and clamped, was being examined by a team of doctors and looked huge next to the others.

Leilani's heart went out not only to the baby girl being examined, but also to her parents who must be worried sick. It was hard to know what problem had caused the medical staff to bring the newborn into the NICU and hover around her, but it had to be a serious and life-threatening condition.

"The Summers baby is right over here," the nurse said, taking them to an isolette near the wall. "Dr. Ernst wants him to stay here for the next few days, maybe even a week."

Leilani peered into the bed, where a tiny baby with tufts of black hair lay. He was bigger than some of the others in the NICU, but he was still just a little peanut.

His lungs, however, seemed to be working, as he grimaced and cried out loud and clear.

Spotting a bruise on his forehead, Leilani furrowed her brow and looked closer. "Is that a result of the delivery?"

"I doubt it," Luke said. "It's probably from the trauma he suffered when his mother was beaten."

"Do you think it will cause him any lasting problems?" She couldn't bring herself to even say *brain damage,* but she figured Luke would read between the lines.

"It's hard to say."

Leilani reached out and gently stroked Michael's downy soft hair. "Poor little guy. He should have been safe and warm in his mother's womb, not attacked by a brute."

"I hear you," Luke said. "And if that bastard, Joel What's-his-ass, were within reach, I'd let him have it."

"That sounds like the old Luke I used to know." She nudged him, and their eyes met and locked. Yet he didn't crack a smile.

She hoped he knew she'd meant that in a good way. Not that she wanted to see him clobber someone in anger, but the old Luke was familiar to her, and she was having to get to know him all over again.

He ran a knuckle along her cheek, sending a tingle of heat to her core and resurrecting old feelings, both physical and emotional.

"I've made a lot of changes in my life," he said, "but the real me is the same. Like it or not."

She suspected he was right about that, and she had to admit that there was a lot she *did* like about him.

More than she should. But rather than comment, she broke eye contact and forced her focus to the baby.

"He's cute, isn't he?"

Luke's hand dropped to his side. "I suppose he is. For a newborn. Most of them look like scrawny extraterrestrials to me."

Moments later, Dr. Ernst, one of the doctors who'd been standing over the isolette of the full-term infant, joined them at Michael's bedside. He was a small man, with blue eyes, a gentle smile and a soft voice. Other than a dash of silver at the temples, he had a youthful appearance. But Leilani had already been convinced of his professional reputation and his medical skill.

As the colleagues shook hands, Dr. Ernst said, "I heard you were involved in this case."

"Sort of," Luke admitted. "This is my friend, Leilani Stephens. She's the guardian of the baby until his mother is able to take care of him."

The newborn specialist seemed to accept Luke's statement and shared his findings and prognosis. "The baby has a significant bruise on his head, but as far as we can tell, there isn't any apparent brain injury. Other than that, he appears fine."

"Thank God." Leilani blew out the breath she'd been holding, releasing a portion of the worry she'd harbored ever since Carrie's attack.

"The extra days in the womb did wonders," Dr. Ernst added, "and he's breathing fine on his own."

Carrie would be pleased to know that—if she ever came to.

"How's his mother doing?" Leilani asked.

"She's still in recovery, but the surgery was uneventful." Dr. Ernst took one last look at the baby. "I'll be by later this evening."

"All right."

After the neonatologist slipped away, the nurse who'd brought them to the baby asked if Leilani would like to hold him.

"I'd love to." Leilani knew how important touch was to an infant, and she'd make sure this little one had plenty of love and cuddling until his mother was able to do the job herself.

The idea that Carrie might never recover fully was too unsettling to ponder.

Luke pulled a rocking chair from the center of the room and offered it to Leilani. She sat, waiting as the nurse carefully wrapped the baby in a flannel blanket and then handed him to her.

She took the child and gently held him close. Then she glanced up and cast a smile at Luke. "It's been a long time since I've held a little one."

"Don't worry," Luke said. "I hear it's like riding a bike."

"Oh yeah?" she asked.

"That's what they tell me." He flashed a crooked smile that crinkled his eyes and sent her pulse rate soaring.

She tried to shrug off the effect he had on her. "I forgot. You've never been around babies."

"Well, that's not exactly true. I've handled my share during my rotations in obstetrics and pediatrics."

And obviously, during those rotations, he'd chosen to specialize in emergency medicine.

"Did you ever consider being a pediatrician?" she asked.

"Nope. Not even for a second. I don't like seeing kids sick or hurt. Nor do I like dealing with their parents. Of course, they don't really like dealing with me, either. From what I've been told more times than I can count, my bedside manner leaves a lot to be desired."

His bedside manner?

She knew what he meant, but her thoughts went in another direction. When it came to being in bed, she had reason to believe his manner was pretty nice.

Unless, like everything else, that had changed, too. But she suspected his skills as a lover had only improved with age.

Curiosity tingled deep in her core.

Given the chance, would she want to find out if that was the case?

She wasn't sure.

Falling to temptation and making love with him would certainly complicate her life. And it wouldn't be wise.

So she shrugged off the possibility and focused her attention on Carrie's baby, a child that would be in Leilani's care for at least a while—maybe even permanently.

He'd stopped crying, lulled by the swaying of the rocker, or maybe by Leilani's embrace and the sound of her voice.

Rocking slowly and holding him close, she whispered, "Welcome to the world, Michael. Your mommy loves you very much."

Carrie should be the one holding him right now, but that wasn't possible.

Leilani studied his sweet face, the rosebud mouth. If he were her son, and he wasn't in intensive care, she would have unwrapped him and counted his fingers and toes as soon as she had the chance.

Like she'd done with Danny.

She glanced at Luke, saw him watching her.

"I'm sorry I missed it," he said.

She suspected where his thoughts had gone. The same place hers had. But she asked anyway. "Missed what?"

"Seeing Danny as a newborn. Watching you with him."

She smiled. "He was a beautiful baby, too."

"No doubt he was. He looks like you."

"But he reminds me of you. More than you can imagine."

She expected him to ask why and in what way, but instead, he merely studied her.

Was he wondering what it would have been like to have been a part of their son's birth?

To drive her to the hospital when her water had broken? To hold her hand through sixteen hours of labor, then watch as their son came into the world and took his first breath?

Would Luke have taken turns walking the floor with Danny at night, when the colic was at its worst?

Would they have lain in bed together, the baby between them, and marveled at the miracle of it all, amazed that their love could create something so precious and perfect?

As supportive as her aunt and grandmother had been, Leilani had felt very much alone in those first few days after childbirth. It had almost seemed as though she and Danny had been missing something.

Or rather someone.

But she hadn't admitted it to herself then. And she didn't want to do so now.

Second-guessing the past wasn't going to do anyone any good.

But what about the future? a small voice asked.

God only knew what tomorrow would bring, and in spite of all her recent prayers, He hadn't whispered a clue.

Chapter Nine

The next day, Leilani got up early and fixed breakfast for Danny and her aunt. As she moved through the small kitchen, setting the table, mixing the batter and flipping pancakes, she plotted out her busy day.

She needed to go to the hospital again, but she didn't want Danny to feel as though she'd completely abandoned him, especially when there was a possibility she might have to raise Carrie's baby as his brother. Getting a new sibling would be an adjustment for a boy who'd always been an only child.

And God knew their family dynamics were already under a strain due to the lie she'd told about his father.

Things did, however, seem to be better between

them. Not as good as they'd been before coming to San Diego, but he'd started talking to her again.

He hadn't said much about Luke, though.

Of course, that was probably because she'd told him not to mention his father in front of Aunt Addie and had insisted that she needed time to reveal Luke's identity herself—time she hadn't yet found.

When Danny entered the kitchen and approached the stove, he peered at the hotcake she was cooking in a cast iron skillet and grinned. "Hey! Thanks, Mom. You made my favorite breakfast."

She caressed the back of his sleep-ruffled hair. "I thought you were due for a nice treat. How'd you sleep?"

"Okay." He plopped into a seat at the dinette table. "After I eat, can I go over to Jake's house to play?"

"Who's Jake?" she asked, as she set a plate of pancakes in front of him.

"Just a kid I met yesterday when Aunt Addie and I went to the Laundromat and washed the towels. His grandma said I could come over and play since we don't have any fun stuff for kids to do around here. And Jake has a new PlayStation with lots of video games and all kinds of other toys."

"Is he visiting his grandmother?" she asked.

"Nope. He lives with her. They have an apartment on the fifth floor."

"I want to talk to Aunt Addie first, then I'll need to meet Jake's grandmother." Leilani was very careful about who she let Danny associate with.

"Jake has a cool video game called Squasher that I've been wanting to check out," Danny said between bites of a syrup-covered pancake. "And he has two controllers, so we can both play at the same time."

Before Leilani could respond, Addie entered the kitchen wearing the worn yellow housecoat and scruffy blue slippers she'd owned for ages. Addie had a birthday coming in September, so shopping for her present would be easy this year.

"Everything smells so good," Addie said. "Especially the coffee."

"Go ahead and take a seat," Leilani told her. "I'll get you a cup."

"Aunt Addie," Danny said, his fork poised and ready to spear another piece of pancake. "Tell my mom that it's okay if I go play with Jake today and that his grandma is super nice."

"He's right. Ruth Goldman is one of the nicest people in the complex. She and her husband live on the fifth floor of this building and are raising their grandson. The boy is mannerly and well-behaved. And he's just a couple of months older than Danny."

Aunt Addie, who wasn't quick to sing anyone's praises, didn't vouch for people very often, so her recommendation went a long way.

"Perhaps you can visit with Ruth while the boys play," Addie suggested. "She's a young grandmother, so you two ought to get along just fine."

Maybe so, but Leilani didn't have time to visit

anyone today. Without access to Carrie's house and the baby supplies that filled the nursery, she'd have to go shopping so little Michael would have everything he needed. By the first of next week—maybe even sooner—she'd need a makeshift nursery for him. Not that there was room for him here.

She'd have to set aside a corner of the room she shared with Danny. Hopefully, having a baby around wouldn't be too much for Addie.

"So, can I, Mom?" Danny asked.

"We'll see." Leilani would have to at least meet Mrs. Goldman before allowing Danny to visit.

"By the way," Addie said, taking a seat next to Danny and holding a chipped blue coffee mug with both hands. "Remember Ethel Danson? The older woman who looked after me when I had that gall-bladder surgery last year?"

"Yes, I do." Ethel had lived next door to Addie for years and had been a good friend. "How is she?"

"Her kids moved her to Huntington Beach a few months ago and put her in a rest home close to their house. They're having a birthday party for her on Sunday afternoon, and I'd like to go. But I'm not comfortable driving all that way to a strange city."

"Would you like me to take you?" Leilani asked.

"If you wouldn't mind. And if you're not too busy with Carrie and the baby at the hospital. Ethel will be ninety. And that's something to celebrate."

"I'll gladly make time, Addie."

Her aunt's craggy smile lit up the small dingy

kitchen. "Thank you, Lani. You've always been so good to me."

"How could I not be? You're a great role model for all of us."

Addie turned to Danny. "Are those flapjacks as yummy as they look?"

He nodded and grinned. "Mmm."

After breakfast had been served and the kitchen put back in order, Leilani let Danny take her upstairs to meet the Goldmans, who were every bit as nice as Addie had said.

Their home, while modest, was cozy and clean. And Jake, a boy who was several inches shorter than Danny, was just as mannerly and polite as Leilani had been told.

Feeling confident that Danny was in good hands, Leilani allowed him to stay and play until after lunch, at which time Addie would take him home.

Then she headed to Horton Plaza, where she purchased the things the baby would need right away, including a bassinet, preemie-size disposable diapers, sleepers, bottles and formula, receiving blankets and a pacifier. The other items—cotton swabs, lotion, baby shampoo and the like—she would pick up later at the grocery store.

After making a good-size dent in her savings account and filling both the trunk and the back seat of Addie's car with supplies, Leilani drove to the hospital and went straight to the ICU to check on Carrie. She didn't have to wait long to be allowed in.

Once at Carrie's bedside, she noted that the

bruising and swelling on her friend's head and face had decreased, and she was beginning to look human again—a fair-haired woman sound asleep. But according to the nurse in charge of her today, there hadn't been a significant change in her condition.

Leilani took Carrie's hand in hers. Several broken nails and bruises on the knuckles were evidence of the struggle she'd put up to protect herself and her baby.

"I wish you'd wake up," Leilani told her, as if she'd just stopped by for a cup of tea. "I can't wait to show you your beautiful baby boy."

A squeeze of the hand would be welcome, something—*anything*—to let Leilani know the words had found their way inside. But there was no response at all.

Still, Leilani didn't let that stop her from having a one-sided conversation with her friend. She hoped her words would trigger something, that news of the baby boy might cause Carrie to wake up, determined to recover.

"Michael only weighs a bit over four pounds, but the doctor says he's going to be fine. All he needs to do is gain weight. Well, that and meet his mommy."

An IV line dripped into Carrie's arm, and monitors kept track of her pulse and blood pressure.

"He has dark hair," Leilani continued. "His eyes are blue now, although they could change as he gets a little older."

She sat like that for a while, holding her friend's

hand and whispering words to touch a mother's heart. Then, when she stood to go, she placed a kiss on Carrie's brow. "I'm going to see Michael now. He loves to be held and rocked. I'll be back later this afternoon and let you know how he's doing."

Then she strode out of the ICU, wishing that Carrie were walking beside her.

When she got to the nursery, an LVN working the desk allowed her inside. After she'd washed up and put on the required gown, she was taken into the NICU and introduced to Karen, the nurse who'd been assigned to Michael that day.

"His condition has been upgraded," Karen said, "but Dr. Ernst wants him to stay in here until he starts gaining weight. That shouldn't take too long. In fact, he could be discharged as early as Monday."

"Good. Is he eating yet?"

"He drank a couple of ounces of formula earlier. He's sleeping now, but if you stick around for a while, you may be able to give him his next feeding."

"Is it okay if I peek at him?" Leilani asked. "I won't wake him."

"Of course."

As Leilani scanned the room, the full-term infant who'd been here last time was missing.

"I hope that little girl who was here yesterday is all right."

The nurse smiled. "Her name is Caitlin, and she only spent one night in here. She's now rooming with her mommy."

"That's good to know." Leilani returned her attention to Michael and watched his little chest rise and fall as he slept.

When he woke, she was allowed to feed him and change his diaper. Then, true to her word, she went back to tell Carrie how well her son was doing today.

On her way out of the hospital, she stopped by the drinking fountain before exiting through the lobby doors. Then she proceeded outside to the parking lot, where she felt the summer breeze on her face, heard birds chirping in the trees. She took a moment to relish the *real* world. A world she hoped Carrie would re-enter soon—fully recovered and able to mother her son.

Footsteps sounded as someone approached, and Luke's voice drew her from her musing. "How's everyone doing today?"

She turned, and a strand of hair blew across her cheek. She brushed it aside and tucked it behind an ear. "Carrie is still the same, but the baby is doing great."

"How about you?" he asked. "How are you holding up?"

"I'm all right." She appreciated the concern that peered through the intensity of his gaze.

"Are you doing well enough to have dinner with me on Friday night?"

"You mean Danny, too?" Leilani assumed he wanted to include their son as he'd done before.

"As much as I'd like to spend more time with him, I thought it would be nice for you to get out. Once that baby is discharged, your life won't be your own any longer."

He had that right, and the thoughtful invitation drew a smile from her heart to her lips. As much as she hated to admit it, she still harbored feelings for him, still longed for his company.

"Sure, Luke. Going to dinner with you would be nice."

Nice? An internal voice that sounded an awful lot like Aunt Addie asked.

Yes. A lot might have changed, but Luke was more attractive than ever and still had a way of stirring her senses, of touching her heart.

And nearly squeezing the love right out of you, that same voice whispered.

On Friday evening, Luke and Leilani were escorted to a linen-draped table at DiCarlo's, an upscale steak house located on the top floor of the Bayside Inn.

Wall-to-wall windows provided a breathtaking view of the Pacific on one side and the city lights on the other, but Luke was too taken by the beautiful woman who'd accompanied him to be more than mildly impressed.

Dressed in a classic black dress and strappy sandals, Leilani turned more than a few heads when they entered the restaurant, and now, under the spell of candlelight, her allure grew steadily.

"This place is incredible," she said. "The service,

the ambiance, the view...." She reached across the white-linen-draped table and placed her hand on Luke's arm. "What a wonderful choice of restaurants. Thanks for bringing me here."

Her smile conveyed appreciation and not a hint of anything sexual, yet her touch sent a rush of heat through his blood that made him yearn for a lot more than a dinner date.

But rather than come across as a geeky teen with a terminal case of puppy love, he shrugged, as though it was no big deal. "I thought you might like it."

"I do. This is a real treat."

It shouldn't be.

Leilani deserved to be wined and dined in places like this.

He studied the candle in the center of the table. The flame, as if mimicking the heated attraction that had always radiated between them, flickered and set off thoughts of romance and happily ever after.

Luke wondered if she felt it, too—the urge to start over, to see where their hearts would lead them.

He'd told himself that nothing could develop between them until she'd forgiven him for her brother's death. But maybe they needed to revive their relationship first, and then forgiveness would follow.

When the wine steward delivered the expensive bottle of merlot Luke had ordered earlier, he poured them each a glass then left them alone again.

Luke lifted his in a toast, and Leilani followed his lead.

To new beginnings, he wanted to say, as the clinking crystal echoed a melodious sound. *And to the pheromones and hormones that hover overhead.*

Instead, he kept his thoughts to himself and took a drink.

She did, too. And when she set down her glass, she blessed him with the hint of a smile. "I'm glad Danny will have a father in his life."

"Me, too. It's tough growing up without one." Luke twirled the stem of his glass, then studied the reflection of the burgundy liquid in the candlelight, before sliding back to her gaze.

"But at least you had Harry Logan," she said.

"That's true." He placed his glass on the table. "Speaking of Harry, he invited me to a picnic at Bayside Park on Sunday afternoon. I'm switching shifts with one of the other residents so I can go. And I'd like you and Danny to join me."

"It sounds like fun. The Logans are wonderful people. I enjoyed meeting them, but I'm afraid we'll have to pass. I promised to drive Aunt Addie to Orange County on Sunday."

"Is there any chance you could take her on another day?"

"I'm afraid not. She's going to attend her friend's birthday party."

He paused for a moment, then brightened. "Why don't I take Danny to the park with me? He enjoyed himself last time."

When Leilani didn't answer right away, Luke

sensed her reluctance. Her determination to protect the boy and keep him under her wing.

"I'm not comfortable letting him go without me," she finally said. "I'll be in Huntington Beach, and that's two hours away."

Luke suspected there was more to it than that. She was probably afraid something would go wrong. And that Luke wouldn't protect him.

Had her thoughts turned to Kami, as his had?

At times, those memories came easy and unbidden, but they were especially strong now. Luke's mind drifted back to the time when he'd been a senior in high school, when he and Leilani had been tiptoeing around a full-blown romance.

She'd been thrilled that day in late May, when Kami had arrived in San Diego, and had looked forward to introducing him to the neighborhood. And the boy who'd grown up on a small island had been eager for adventure.

Everything about the inner city had been exciting to the bright-eyed fourteen-year-old. He'd just entered a brand-new world, a fascinating urban wonderland he was determined to explore.

Like Leilani, Kami was bright and every bit as naive. It didn't take Luke five minutes to make that assessment. Nor did it take Kami long to gravitate toward Luke, much to Addie's chagrin.

Luke, who'd been used to a different kind of fan club, found it unnerving to have someone young and innocent look at him in hero worship. Yet he didn't have the heart to tell Kami to stop dogging him around the neighborhood.

In retrospect, there was something to be said about having street smarts, and Luke believed Kami's innocence had played a part in his death. So he would make sure Danny learned to be aware and savvy— not sheltered his entire life like Kami had been. But first he'd have to work on Leilani.

"If you let Danny go to the picnic at the park with me," Luke said, expecting her to imply that she still held him responsible for her brother's death, "I'll protect him."

Leilani arched a brow, as though skeptical.

"I'm a doctor, remember? And if an emergency comes up, I can handle it."

"I realize that," she said. "But it's been just the two of us for so long that it's hard letting go."

Good. The Kami thing hadn't come up.

"Danny is already eleven, and before you know it, he'll be a teenager. Besides, he'll not only be with me, but with a retired detective. And I can almost guarantee there will be a couple of off duty firefighters and police officers there. Who better to look after him?"

As silence and indecision stretched between them, Leilani considered Luke's words.

She supposed it wouldn't hurt to let Luke take his son. The park at the Marina was safe. And Danny would be with people who could protect him.

When it came to her son, there were times when

she failed to access the skills and knowledge she'd acquired along with her degree in social work, and this was one of them. Luke was right. She needed to let Danny grow up.

Still, she couldn't help thinking of Luke's negligence the night he was supposed to be looking out for Kami. To this day, she never understood why she hadn't followed her intuition, why she'd even introduced Kami to Luke in the first place.

Back then, Leilani might have loved Luke, but he'd had a rebellious edge and an untamed side she hadn't wanted Kami to come into contact with.

Yet, as she was leaving for a weekend tour of the college she would attend in the fall, she'd asked Luke to keep her brother company while she was gone. He'd agreed, then took Kami to a wild party where tragedy struck.

But there was no reason to rehash those events now, twelve years later.

Besides, Luke had changed.

Danny would be safe with him, wouldn't he?

"All right," she said. "I'll let him go to the picnic with you."

"You won't be sorry." Luke reached out, covering her left hand with his. His thumb caressed her skin and sent a heated tingle through her nervous system, triggering a sense of emptiness in her core. A slow and growing ache that, when he slowly removed his hand, only grew stronger. "I'll stick to him like a cornerback on a wide receiver."

"I know you'll look out for him. But *no* football. It's too dangerous."

"Okay. It's a deal. I'm just glad you'll let him go."

Leilani took a slow sip of the merlot, relishing the smooth taste. As she lowered the glass, she studied Luke over the rim.

In this lovely setting, in the soft, glowing candle-light, she couldn't deny the romantic vibes that were stimulated by more than the ambiance of DiCarlo's. Would they follow her and Luke out the door?

Undoubtedly. And she suspected that if she let herself go, she could fall in love with this man all over again.

Of course, thoughts of love and romance were easy to imagine on an enchanting night like this, so she swept aside the possibilities, deciding to let the evening and the magic run its course.

After dinner—shrimp scampi for her and prime rib for him—Leilani had to agree that the renowned chef at DiCarlo's had prepared one of the finest meals she'd ever eaten. And that this five-star dining experience with Luke was one of the most enjoyable she'd ever had.

For dessert, they shared a slice of "tropical delight," a delicious cheesecake that had a dash of fresh coconut added to the crust and was topped with a chunky fruit blend of pineapple, papaya and mango. The maitre d' had been right, the popular choice was tantalizing from the first bite to the last.

After Luke paid the bill, he escorted Leilani to the

parking lot, where the whisper of a breeze carried the scent of the ocean. Overhead, a new moon and a blanket of flickering stars blessed the night, and the magic that had been brewing all evening grew stronger.

Luke walked her to the passenger side of his vehicle, then paused. "Thanks for coming with me tonight."

Leilani nudged his arm, like she used to when they'd been young, and smiled. "Don't thank me. I don't usually go to such classy restaurants."

Yet it had been more than the view or the food that had touched her heart. It had been sharing it all with Luke.

As if under the spell of a fairy godmother with a romantic bent, her hand lifted, and she skimmed her fingers along Luke's cheek.

He placed his hand over hers, holding her touch. Possessing it.

And her.

Their gazes locked, and magic consumed the night. Desire took center stage. Her fingers pressed into his cheek, gentle but insistent, and she drew his lips to hers.

With her arms around his neck, and her breasts pressed lightly against his chest, she leaned into him, her mouth claiming his.

All the love she'd once had, all the desire they'd once shared, sparked to life and the kiss deepened. Lips parted and tongues met, seeking, tasting, taunting.

As a fire inside heated with a seductive roar, she

whimpered, and her hands threaded through his hair, pulling him closer. Deeper.

When Luke broke the kiss, she wanted to object, to tell him she hadn't had enough of him yet. But he didn't let go.

Holding her tight, he pressed his lips against her hair. His breathing was ragged, and when he whispered, his voice bore the throaty weight of desire.

"Come home with me."

Chapter Ten

Come home with me.

Luke's words reverberated in the night air, as he waited for Leilani's response. She neither pulled away nor answered, but he could feel the emotional tug-of-war going on with each beat of her heart.

He slowly released her, even though he damn near ached to draw her back into an embrace, to kiss her again and to forget he'd mentioned doing anything more than necking in a public parking lot. He wouldn't reel in his words, though. Nor would he try to sway her to do anything she wasn't ready for.

Their gazes remained their only connection, as his pulse throbbed with need. It was more than lust or obsession fueling his desire for the woman who'd stolen his heart at first sight and had never relinquished it.

Did she know what she did to him? Or how vulnerable he felt right now?

If she told him it was too soon, or that she needed to get back to her aunt's place for whatever reason, he could handle it. But if she didn't want to take a chance on him again, it would be a bitter pill to swallow.

Did he dare spill his guts and lay his innermost thoughts and desires on the line?

No. Not unless she did so first.

And even then, he wasn't sure he knew what he felt for her. Or what he was able to admit to.

She cleared her throat and forced a swallow, yet she still didn't respond.

He sensed a battle raging and the little angel on her shoulder putting up one hell of a fight. But the fact that she hadn't managed to tell him "no" yet proved that the white-winged warrior in a choir robe didn't have the advantage.

"You have no idea how tempted I am to say yes," she finally said.

Oh, yes he did, and he ought to puff up and be happy about it. But for some reason he felt like a crafty snake slithering up an apple tree.

"If we *do* go to your house," she said, "it will change a lot of things."

Personally, he thought things needed a good shake-up. That he could use a second chance. But he wouldn't push or press her to do anything she didn't want to do.

That had always been his philosophy with her—maybe because he knew, deep inside, that he didn't deserve a woman like her. In fact, he had half a notion to laugh it off and say, "I was just joking. I knew all along you wouldn't be up for a roll in the sheets."

But just as the notion began to have merit, she leaned into him.

He slipped an arm around her. "If you need more time, I understand. It's okay."

She didn't pull away, and when she spoke, her voice was a whisper-soft caress. "You said that to me before. That night at the beach. Remember?"

He *had* said it. How could he not remember the night they'd set off fireworks of their own? It had been the Fourth of July, yet at the time he'd thought of it as the First of Forever.

But forever hadn't been in their cards.

Not then anyway. And maybe not now.

"I meant what I said back then," he admitted.

She rested her head against his shoulder. "I know."

"I still have feelings for you," he added. "And I'd like to see what happens between us. But if you're not ready…"

She turned her body, so that they were completely facing one another. "I have feelings for you, too, Luke, and you don't know how badly I *want* to go home with you."

If he hadn't been hanging on her every word and looking in her eyes, he would have glanced up and thanked his lucky stars. "I'd like that, too."

"But I can't spend the night."

"No problem. Just say the word and I'll take you home. Even if you change your mind."

"You've always let me call the shots when it came to this sort of thing." She brushed a kiss across his lips, light and sweet. "And I appreciate it. It's just that I'm a little…"

"Scared?" he asked. She'd felt that way before.

"Not really. I'm just a little nervous. It's been a long time. And I might have forgotten how."

He chuckled, a crooked grin tugging at his lips. "I hear it's like riding a bike."

"That's what you said about holding a baby."

"Yes, I did. And sure enough, when the nurse placed that little guy in your arms, you slipped right into maternal mode."

They stood silent for a while, the stars watching over them.

When they'd met as teenagers, Luke had already slept with several girls, but Leilani had been a virgin. Still, he hadn't pressed her for more than she was ready to give, even though there had been times he'd gone home blue-balled and aching. And he'd do so again tonight, even if it damn near killed him—which it might.

Every lover he'd ever had—before or since—had fallen short in one way or another.

"I don't want you to have any regrets," he told her. "So, we can take things slow and easy."

"All right."

He assumed she meant that they could start dating, but that making love was something he'd have to wait for.

So he nearly dropped to his knees when she added, "Let's go to your house."

If God struck him down in the morning, Luke would die a happy man.

He placed a kiss on her brow, then opened the door of his Expedition and waited for her to climb in. As she did, the future, which had already been on a professional fast-track, seemed brighter than he'd ever imagined.

Yet on the way to his place in Bayside, he waited for something to go wrong. For the little angel to rally and convince Leilani to change her mind.

It would take nearly fifteen minutes to get to Playa del Sol, the condominium complex in which he'd made his home. And that was plenty of time for the kiss they'd shared to turn into a memory and the heat of passion to cool—at least on her part.

But he'd meant what he'd said. If she changed her mind, he wouldn't try to sway her one way or the other.

Even if it killed him to let her go.

Playa del Sol, with its white stucco buildings and red tile roofs, was a lovely, Spanish-style complex that sat on the bay. Even at night, it was easy to see the well-manicured grounds adorned with palms, tropical plants and flowers.

A wave of nervous anticipation surged through

Leilani. She hoped it hadn't been a mistake, coming here with Luke. Yet when he opened the front door and allowed her inside, she entered without hesitation and scanned his domain.

The living room, with its hardwood entry and Berber carpet, was clean and spacious. The few pieces of furniture, a black leather sofa, a glass-topped coffee table and a chrome floor lamp, were lost in the room. Other than a plasma television that hung over the fireplace like a piece of art, the stark white walls were bare.

A sliding door led to the patio, where a sturdy, wrought iron table and chairs rested. It was dark outside, but as she approached the glass, she could see the lights of a ship out on the bay. "I'll bet this view is beautiful during the day."

"It is. I know it isn't much now, but as soon as I can pay down my student loans a bit more, I'm going to hire a decorator."

She suspected he wanted a home he could be proud of, a place that was miles away from the run-down apartment in which he'd grown up. He'd done well for himself and had every right to be proud of his home.

She glanced over her shoulder and caught his gaze. There was so much about Luke to like, to admire. To be drawn to.

He stood about ten feet away, giving her space and freedom, yet she recognized passion smolder-ing in his eyes.

"You're not making this easy for me," she said, as

she turned completely and slowly closed the gap between them.

"Sorry. I've been trying my best to be a gentleman, which doesn't come easy for me."

There was something to be said about a man who respected a woman. It was one of the traits that had endeared Luke to her in the past. One of many, actually.

"For what it's worth," he said, "I've missed you."

"I've missed you, too." She slipped easily into his arms and rested her face against his cheek. She inhaled deeply, savoring the scent of man and musk and the light splash of an ocean-fresh aftershave.

Never had she felt so alive, so aware of herself as a woman.

As he held her close, her breasts splayed against his chest, their hearts beating in harmony, she felt protected and safe. More so than she ever had before.

When she brushed a kiss across his cheek, he tilted his face, offering his mouth instead. Her lips parted, and as his tongue sought hers, she let go of any reservations she might have been clinging to and lost herself in his arms.

Their breaths mingled, their tongues mated and heat exploded in a sexual rush, as they explored each other with hungry hands, stroking and caressing.

When Luke reached her breasts, he worshipped them with an expert touch. His thumbs taunted her nipples, and they contracted in response. An emptiness built in her core, a growing need only Luke could fill.

Leilani had never felt such a carnal craving, and there was no turning back. She wanted Luke, wanted this.

Now.

But then he removed his lips from hers and put a stop to the intoxicating assault on her body, breaking the kiss and tearing a whimper from her.

She feared her knees would buckle and she held on tight. "Is something wrong?"

"No, not at all." His voice, as well as his breathing, was ragged with desire. "I just want to make love with you in a real bed this time."

Right now, Leilani wouldn't have minded a blanket on the sand, the sky, their only covers—just like their first time. And if truth be told, she was so caught up in lust, so aroused and ready, that she would have let him take her on the floor.

"Come with me." He took her hand and led her into a large master bedroom.

As they neared a four-poster, king-size bed draped with a blue plaid comforter, she withdrew her hand and turned, presenting her back and lifting her hair so he could help her remove the dress. After he'd unzipped her, he placed a kiss on her neck, then pushed the fabric from her shoulders. She peeled it off the rest of the way, letting it slide down and puddle on the floor.

"Aw, Lani," he said, lapsing into a nickname her family had used. One he'd never used before, although she'd told him he could. "You're more beautiful than I remembered."

Her cheeks warmed and she smiled. "You'll see a few stretch marks that weren't there before."

"Then I'll make it a point to kiss each one."

She stood before him in a black lace bra and panties, yet bolstered by the unspoken love in his sweet words and the glaze of desire in his eyes, she no longer felt the least bit vulnerable or self-conscious.

Instead, she was eager to shed her underwear and remove his clothing, too. To feel her skin against his.

Nothing else seemed to matter.

She cupped his cheeks and kissed his mouth, then reached for the buttons of his shirt. Within moments, they were both naked.

Luke loved her with his hands and his mouth, and with each touch, each kiss, each flick of the tongue, he drove her wild with need.

She was lost in an intoxicating swirl of heat and desire. When she feared her knees would no longer hold her, he seemed to sense it and lifted her in his arms. Then he carried her to his bed, where he finished what he'd begun, kissing her where she'd never been kissed, loving her in a way she'd never been loved.

By the time it seemed she would die from want of him, he reached into the drawer of the nightstand and drew out a small packet. After protecting them both, he returned to bed and lay beside her, braced on one elbow. His eyes seemed to ask if she was sure. And she was.

As he rolled and hovered over her, she opened for

him, placing her hands on his hips and guiding him home—where it seemed he belonged.

He entered her, working his magic, and she was caught up in the tantalizing, in-and-out sensation. She arched to meet each thrust until they reached a mind-shattering peak. As a powerful climax rocked her to the core, she cried out in pure delight.

When the last wave of pleasure ebbed, she held on tight, cheek to cheek, heart to heart—afraid to move and break the tenuous connection.

She'd been right. Making love had changed the dynamics between them, but she wasn't sure in which way.

As he raised his head, his hair brushed across her cheek. She dared to open her eyes and found him watching her. The emotion that welled in her heart was almost overwhelming.

She'd only had one other lover, but that had been years ago, and right now, she couldn't quite remember his name, let alone recall what they'd shared.

She just hoped Luke wasn't making his own comparisons. And if he was, she hoped...

"Are you okay?" he asked.

"Yes, I'm fine." No, that wasn't true. She was better than fine. She was completely sated.

And enamored by it all.

Her mouth opened to admit it, then she clamped it shut, waiting to gain a sense of his reaction first.

"Fine, huh?" Luke rolled to the side, taking her with him. Making love had been more than he'd hoped for, and he was so sexually spent that he could scarcely find his voice.

And she'd said it was *fine.*

Under normal circumstances his ego might have taken a direct hit with such a bland comment. But the whimpers she'd made and the scratch marks her nails had left on his back told him it had been much better for her than that.

He wouldn't question her about it any further. In fact, if he did, he wasn't sure what to say. He wasn't the kind to lie around and bask in the sexual afterglow, so he didn't have any scripts for this.

But tonight was different, and he had no urge to get up at all.

Damn. She'd been right. Making love had changed things; it certainly had changed him.

Looking at her, skin flushed from passion, hair splayed upon his pillow, he realized all he'd been given. All he could lose if she chose to end things before they got started.

A loose strand of hair had fallen across her brow. He brushed it away, leaving a kiss in its place.

Was-it-good-for-you questions were typical after sex. Sure, he wanted to know that it had been good for her, but more than that, he felt as though he had to make up for the last time, as special as it had been for him.

Twelve years ago, she'd cried afterward, which had crushed him. But she'd sworn everything was okay, that she was just overwhelmed by it all. He'd believed her, yet more than ever he'd been filled with the need to protect her.

Yet two days later, he'd let her down. And Kami had died as a result.

Luke may not have received her forgiveness yet, but he'd been given hope. Hope that they might start dating again, that someday they might create a family together.

That someday she'd accept his apology.

Trying to get his answer in a roundabout way, he asked, "Any regrets?"

"No."

"Good."

"Can I use your bathroom?" she asked. "I'd like to freshen up before going home."

He wanted to ask her to stay for a while longer, to throw caution to the wind and spend the night, to sleep in his arms until dawn. To let him try and speak from his heart.

But he wouldn't.

Instead, he got out of bed and led her to the bathroom. "Let me know if you need anything."

She blessed him with a smile. "You met all my needs a few minutes ago."

Then she closed the door, leaving him to bask in the waning afterglow alone.

Leilani had wanted to spend the night wrapped in Luke's arms, but she couldn't come trotting home in the morning. There would be too many questions to dodge, too many answers to skate around.

They drove through the quiet city streets, each lost in the after-the-loving awkwardness until they approached the Eberly Arms.

"Just drop me off here," she said.

"No way. I'm going to make sure you get home safely."

"But once I'm in the garage—"

"Don't even think about it, honey. There's a semblance of security in place here, which is probably fine, but no one knows how rough the city streets can be at this time of night better than I do."

She couldn't argue. And secretly, she appreciated his concern, his determination to protect her. But what he didn't realize was that she'd grown adept at protecting herself. With her job as a counselor, she never knew when she might be stalked by an angry husband or boyfriend looking for a woman who'd gone underground and was living in a shelter.

So she'd honed her sense of awareness when it came to her surroundings. And to ensure that she could keep herself and Danny safe, she'd taken self-defense courses and worked out regularly back in L.A.

Luke pulled up along the curb and parked, then walked with her to the gated garage door. She punched in the code and, when the doors swung open, walked with him to the elevator.

"Thank you for a great evening," she said.

"My pleasure." He tossed her a grin, suggesting he'd liked the after dinner part of the date best of all.

As they waited for the elevator doors to open, he reached for her hand. "Don't forget about the picnic on Sunday."

"I won't forget. My aunt and I will be leaving around eleven, so if you'll be home, I'll bring Danny to you before we go."

"Of course. I guess you won't need directions, now that you know where I live."

She cast him a smile. "At two-twenty-six Acapulco Court. In Bayside, right next to the park at the marina."

"And you've got my phone number."

She patted her purse. "It's programmed into my cell."

"Good." He gave her hand a squeeze. "I'll call you tomorrow."

"Okay."

Then when the elevator let them out at the fourth floor, he gave her a promise-filled kiss, one she had to tear herself away from.

"Thanks again," she said, stepping into the hall and leaving him in the elevator. "For everything."

Her appreciation went beyond that for a lovely dinner, although she wasn't exactly sure what she was thanking him for.

Taking her to the moon and back, she supposed.

He held the elevator open and watched until she let herself into Addie's apartment and shut the door.

It had been a wonderful evening, but the same sense of guilt that had haunted her the first time she'd made love to Luke struck with a vengeance now that she was home.

Addie called out from her bedroom. "Is that you, Lani?"

"Yes, I'm sorry for waking you."

"That's okay. I wouldn't have been able to rest easy until you were home." Addie's light clicked on from her room down the hall. "For goodness' sake, Lani. It's after midnight. Where've you been?"

"I had dinner with a friend. Remember? We had a lot of catching up to do, and one thing led to another." It was the truth. All of it.

Yet in her heart, she knew it was merely one of those cleverly disguised comments that could be taken two ways. A lie masquerading as truth. Part of her wanted to come clean tonight, to tell Addie exactly where she'd been and with who.

Not what she'd done, of course. Some things were too special, too private, to share.

Besides, all she wanted right now was to lie in the dark and relive every touch, every kiss, every sweet moment she'd experienced in Luke's arms.

Telling Addie tonight would ruin the memory, so she would do it tomorrow. Or better yet, maybe Sunday. She and Addie would be on the road together.

All Leilani had to do was figure out a way to set things straight, to tell Addie that Luke was Danny's father and that he wanted to develop a relationship with his son, that Luke was her lover and was going to be a part of her life.

Addie wasn't going to be at all pleased to learn the truth, but it had to be told.

Besides, even God knew Sundays were the best days for confessions and absolution.

Chapter Eleven

Leilani drove up Interstate 5 on the way to Huntington Beach, her eyes on the road, her mind on the conversation she planned to have with her aunt.

Addie, wearing her newest pair of blue slacks and a matching butterfly print blouse, gazed out the window at a religious mural painted on the side of a passing eighteen-wheeler. The colorful artwork depicted man's fall from grace and redemption.

A coincidence?

Or a sign that the time had come to confess?

Thus far, the trip had been quiet and uneventful, but that was about to change.

Leilani had planned to get a few more miles down the road before broaching the subject, yet as she passed Solana Beach, she realized she'd have to say something pretty soon—before her luck ran out, like it almost had this morning at breakfast.

She, Addie and Danny had been seated at the small dinette table in the kitchen, eating and making the usual small talk.

"Danny," Addie said, "there may not be any boys and girls your age at Ethel's party, but I'm sure they'll have plenty of cake and ice cream."

"That's okay," Danny said. "I'm not going with you guys. I'm going to a picnic at the park instead."

"You are?" Addie shot a quizzical look at Leilani. "With whom?"

Leilani took a sip of tea. "A friend of mine."

"Which friend?" Addie asked, as she spread a dollop of marmalade on her toast. "The one you had dinner with the other night?"

"Yes, and a couple of others you don't know. Kay Logan is a volunteer at a local shelter. She and her husband are hosting a potluck at Bayside Park. Since several other children will be there, I'm sure Danny will have a much better time."

Addie lifted her coffee mug. "You're probably right."

Leilani nearly blew out a sigh of relief, proud of the way she'd skated around the truth—until she glanced at Danny and read the disapproval in his frown.

As he got up to put his cereal bowl in the sink, she took him aside. "Come with me. I want to talk to you about the rules for the park. And then we need to get your things together."

He seemed to realize that she wanted to talk privately, so he followed her into the living room without a complaint.

"Just for the record," she said, "I'm going to explain everything to Aunt Addie today. On the drive to Orange County."

"Okay. Does that mean I can tell everyone at the park that Luke is my dad?"

She wanted to tell him to wait, but that wouldn't be fair. Besides, with the word out, it would force her to follow through on her promise. "Of course you can, although you might want to talk to Luke about it first and make sure he's ready for the announcement. But I have a feeling he'll be delighted."

Danny grinned. "Cool. I know I promised not to tell anyone, but I already said something to Jake."

"I wish you wouldn't have."

"Jake is my best friend, Mom."

Already? They'd only met a couple of days ago. But she supposed it wasn't unusual for children to bond quickly. Besides, she'd been pretty particular about who he socialized with, so he hadn't claimed too many best friends over the course of his life.

She forced a smile. "Okay. I understand your excitement."

Then she kissed him on the forehead and helped him pack a few things to take to the park: a tube of sunblock, a bottle of water, a windbreaker in case it got unseasonably cool and a change of clothes.

While Addie had dressed for the party, Leilani had driven Danny to his father's house, then returned to pick up her aunt. Now they were on their way.

She'd felt pretty good about leaving Luke and Danny together and tried to shake off any lingering worry. Luke was proving to be considerate and thoughtful. Besides, as he'd reminded her, he *was* a doctor. And Nick Granger was a detective and Joe Davenport was a fireman. So he'd been right. If anything were to happen, Danny would be in good hands.

As they neared the Carlsbad city limits, she figured it was now or never. Besides, they were only about an hour away from Huntington Beach, and Addie would need some cooldown time. No need going into the party in a bad mood.

"I have something to tell you," Leilani said. "And it isn't going to be easy for me. Nor will it please you."

Addie turned in her seat, her steel-blue eyes zeroing in on Leilani.

Just get it over with, her conscience ordered. *Spit it out.*

Leilani cleared her throat, her fingers tightening their hold on the steering wheel. "I told you a lie twelve years ago, and I'm afraid I've been perpetuating it and building upon it."

"You *lied* to me?" Addie's shattered expression was nearly reason to change her mind, to say April

Fools. But the family prided itself on honesty, and this wasn't a joke.

"Yes, I did. Back when I was in high school. And in trying to maintain that lie, I let it evolve over the years."

"What in the world did you lie about?"

"I knew you didn't like Luke Wynter. And I went against your wishes and saw him behind your back."

"That hellion?"

"It was wrong, I know. And at first, it was just an attraction, but over the course of my senior year, I fell in love with him."

Addie made a snort-like humph. "You were only a child back then. What did you know about love?"

"I was seventeen—going on eighteen. And I've never felt the same way about a man since."

"Not even Danny's father?" Addie asked. "The sailor?"

"I'm afraid that was the biggest deception of all."

"What do you mean?"

She continued to stare straight ahead, glad to have something to focus on other than her aunt's face. "After Kami died, the entire family was devastated, and we blamed Luke. Then, when I found out I was pregnant, I didn't want to add insult to injury. I was afraid to tell you that Luke was the father of my baby."

"Oh, dear God. The man who killed Kami is Danny's father?"

"Luke *didn't* kill Kami. The police report was clear about that. Kami went to a party with Luke and got high on PCP. Then, when trying to get away from the police during the bust, he was struck by a speeding car."

"How do you think your sweet little brother got a hold of that drug?"

When Leilani didn't answer, Addie clucked her tongue. "Luke gave it to him, Lani. And you can't convince me otherwise. Kami never would have done something like that on his own. And he wouldn't have run from the police, either. Luke put him up to that."

At a time like this, Leilani wished she would have let Luke give her the details of her brother's death. Not that she believed he was any less negligent or any less responsible, but at least she'd be able offer some answers and put out a few fires.

"I'm sorry for not being honest, Aunt Addie. At the time, I was afraid the truth would destroy you, Grandma and Grandpa. And since I had no intention of ever seeing Luke again, I figured the lie wouldn't matter."

"Lies *always* matter." Addie crossed her arms and scowled. Then, as if a lightbulb clicked on in her mind, her lips parted. "Oh my God. You're seeing him again. He's the friend you were with the other night. The friend you asked to look after Danny today."

For a moment, Addie's comments caused Leilani to question her decision to become involved with Luke again, to open her heart to him and allow him to be a part of their son's life. But she shoved aside her uneasiness and rallied, determined that she'd done the right thing, that she had nothing to feel guilty about. That she couldn't hold Kami's death against him forever.

Luke had changed.

"It's been twelve years, Addie. Luke has not only grown up and turned his life around, he's also gone to med school and become a doctor."

"That's supposed to make me feel better about all of this?"

Bottom line, there was only one thing Leilani would apologize for. "I'm sorry I lied to you, Aunt Addie."

"So am I." Her aunt, her father's only living relative, the woman who'd raised him, turned her head and stared at the road.

Leilani's stomach knotted. "Will you forgive me?"

Addie remained stiff and frozen for what seemed like the longest time, then she turned to Leilani. "You know, when I was a little girl and did something wrong, I would apologize to my father. And do you know what he would say to me?"

Leilani didn't know much about the man who was her father's grandfather, and she slowly shook her head.

Addie cleared her throat, her expression unreadable, her eyes filled with pain. "No, Adelaide. I will *not* accept your apology, because you never should have done it in the first place."

Apparently, that was Addie's way of saying Leilani was going to have to wait a long time to get back in her good graces. That forgiveness wouldn't come easy—if at all.

Either way, Luke was a part of Leilani's life again, which was another hurdle Addie would have to get over.

"Believe it or not," Leilani said, "Luke has changed. And like it or not, Danny deserves to know his father."

"How can you forgive him so easily?"

How could she not? He'd changed. And he'd told her he was sorry.

They rode along in silence for a while, then Addie clucked her tongue again. "I can't believe you left Danny with him. What if something happens?"

"Nothing will happen." Her words came out strong. Assured.

So why did she still feel so uneasy about leaving Danny in Luke's care?

At Bayside Park, Luke waited for Danny to get out of the vehicle.

He nodded at the red-and-black canvas backpack that Danny was leaving in the car. "Don't you need that?"

"No. It's just sunblock and stuff. And my mom smeared it all over me before we got to your house. Can't we just leave it here? Bringing that thing makes me feel like a baby."

It hadn't been such a long time ago that Luke had been a boy. Although it might have been nice to have had someone give a damn about his health and well-being when he was eleven, he could see why Danny might be embarrassed to drag along what seemed like a diaper bag.

The rebel in him wanted to say, "I hear ya, kid.

Screw it. Just leave it in here." But the doctor in him
thought it best to honor Leilani's wishes. "I could
give you an hour lecture on the dangers of ultravio-
let rays, but I'd rather not. Trust me on this. Let me
carry that bag. It'll please your mom if she knows we
brought it."

Danny passed the backpack to Luke. After
slipping his arm through one of the straps, Luke
locked up the Expedition.

As they stepped onto the park lawn, Danny asked,
"Are they here yet?"

Luke spotted Kay and Harry near the gazebo,
where they were draping a red-and-white checkered
cloth over a picnic table. He gave Danny a nudge,
then pointed. "There they are."

"I don't see any kids with them."

"That's probably because we're early."

Luke had been happy to see Danny this morning
and to be able to take him to Harry's picnic, but he
hadn't known quite what to do with him after Leilani
dropped him off and left. They'd watched a little TV
and made small talk about the Angels and the
Dodgers, then drifted to an upcoming pre-season
football game between the Raiders and the Chargers.
Still, the conversation lagged at times. So Luke had
decided to head to the park early.

"There were only babies last time," Danny
reminded him. "I sure hope bigger kids come today."

"They will. I talked to my friend, Joe Davenport, last night. And he told me he was bringing his

son Bobby. You met Joe at Harry's house. He was the fireman."

"Yeah, I remember. He was pretty cool. He's a good football player, too."

"Joe told me that Brett Tanner has his son this weekend, so that makes another boy about your age."

"What's his name?"

"Justin."

As they neared the table, Kay glanced up and brightened. "Well, look who's here."

"How are you doing, Kay?" Luke offered her a hug. "Are you feeling any better?"

"Actually, I'm doing great. My doctor changed my medication, and it's made all the difference in the world."

As he released Kay, he shook Harry's hand in greeting.

"I can't believe it," Harry said. "You're the first to arrive for a change. That's one for the *Guinness Book of Records.*"

Usually Luke was the last to arrive and the first to leave, but he'd had reason to be early today.

Luke grinned and placed a hand on his son's shoulder. "You remember my friend, Danny, don't you?"

"Of course." Kay welcomed the boy with a smile. "I'm so glad you could join us again."

Danny nudged Luke. "You can tell them, if you want to."

"Tell us what?" Kay asked.

Luke was at a loss. "I'm not sure I know what you mean."

Danny motioned with his fingers, letting Luke know he had a secret.

"Excuse us," Luke said to his friends, "will you?"

Kay nodded. "Of course."

Luke took Danny aside and leaned his ear toward the boy who cupped his mouth and whispered, "You know. The secret about me and you. Mom is going to tell Aunt Addie on the way to the birthday party today. So if you want, you don't have to say I'm just your friend."

Something inside Luke's heart warmed, as Danny made the first step toward a real father/son relationship. And he wished he'd been ready for it, that he'd known exactly what the boy had been hinting at and hadn't needed to be told.

"Ohhh," Luke said, drawing out the word. *"That* one. I'm sorry. Sometimes doctors have to be really good at keeping people's secrets, so I didn't want to blurt out anything without being sure it was okay with you." Luke straightened, then stroked the back of his son's hair. "I'm glad I can reveal the good news."

Danny shrugged, yet a smile tugged at his lips. "Me, too. But I'll probably never become a doctor."

"Why's that?"

"Because I'm not so good at keeping secrets. I told my friend Jacob all about you."

A sense of pride swelled, joining the warmth in Luke's heart and adding to the fullness he'd been feeling all morning. He wanted details and was tempted to ask what Danny had told his friend, what he thought about the E.R. doctor who'd bumped the phantom Navy SEAL off his pedestal. But he'd be damned if he'd pry.

Instead, they returned to the Logans, and Luke explained what all the whispering was about. "Calling Danny my friend wasn't exactly right. Actually, he's my son. We're just getting to know each other, but we plan to be friends, too."

"That's wonderful news." Kay wrapped an arm around Danny. "Let me be the first to welcome you to our extended family."

"Thanks." Danny glanced up at Luke and beamed.

Harry greeted the boy with a shake of the hand. "You have no idea how happy I am to hear that, Danny. Your dad has a heck of a lot going for him. But there was one thing missing—a son."

"Yeah, well I've been missing a dad, too."

Before long, everyone else began to filter in, and Luke made a point of introducing Danny to each person. If they'd been surprised about the son Luke hadn't mentioned in eleven years, they didn't show it.

As soon as Bobby Davenport and Justin Tanner arrived, Luke introduced the boys, then asked if they'd like to throw the Frisbee back and forth with him. It wasn't easy for a kid to make new friends, so he was pleased to see the ploy work.

Before long, the two other fathers joined in.

All three boys were having a blast, but the smile

plastered on Danny's face—so much like his mother's—was enough to make Luke look forward to fatherhood. And to accept the inevitable changes in his life that would go along with it.

While Danny chased a throw that had gone astray, Luke took a time-out to go to the center of the park and get a drink from the fountain that had been built on a base made of rock and concrete. The water came out in a swift, cool flow, and splashed down his throat, quenching his thirst.

He straightened just as Danny came trotting back with the blue plastic disc. With his free hand, he swiped the sweat from his brow, leaving a dirty smudge in its place.

Luke wasn't sure what Leilani would say about the dirt and grass stains on the knees of Danny's khaki slacks. But she probably knew how competitive their son was. After all, he was all over the grass playing field, chasing after the Frisbee, snagging it in the air or diving for it before it hit the ground.

A surge of delight rushed through Luke, and he couldn't help smiling to himself. Danny might resemble his mother in looks, but in many other ways he was a chip off the old block.

If Leilani were here, she might try to rein him in. But what she didn't know wouldn't hurt her.

When Nick Granger arrived with his wife Hailey and little Harry, he was quick to join the group. "Hey, how about a game of Ultimate Frisbee."

"What's that?" Danny asked.

"Well, if you like soccer, basketball and football," Nick said, "you'll love this game. It's played with a disc rather than a ball."

When they all agreed that it sounded like fun, Nick added, "The object is to pass the disc from teammate to teammate. You're not allowed to run with the disc until it's caught in the end zone. If a defensive player intercepts or blocks the disc, they get to pick it up and immediately switch to offense, trying to score in their own end zone. You'll get the hang of it pretty quick."

Then he went on to explain the rules to the boys in more detail and a few tricks in passing. "Most newbies to the game can only throw backhand, which puts you at a disadvantage. The trick is to develop a solid forehand, too."

You'd better pass on Ultimate, a small voice told Luke. *You promised not to let Danny play.*

Yeah, he'd promised. But Leilani had been talking about football, and this wasn't the same thing. Ultimate was a non-contact sport.

Sure, the guys were competitive, and every once in a while they got a little carried away and there were a few collisions and tumbles. But the grass made the ground soft. Besides, Bobby and Justin were going to play. How could Luke tell Danny to sit it out?

Determined not to steal the happiness from his son's face, Luke shut out the pesky voice that reminded him of the promise he'd made Leilani, reminding himself that she went to the extreme when it came to protecting the boy.

Zack Henderson, who'd just arrived with his pretty wife and daughters, was quick to jump in the game. "Luke, why don't you and Brett be captains. Nick and I got to pick our teams last time."

"All right. I'll start by choosing Danny."

His son beamed, then nudged him. "We'll whip 'em. Won't we?"

A sense of camaraderie and family pride washed over Luke, and before long, the teams had been chosen and paper cups had been used to mark the end zones. Then they lined up and the disc was put into play.

The game went on for about thirty minutes or so, long enough for Luke to marvel at the athletic ability Danny had inherited. The boy had good hands and was fast on his feet.

When Harry and Kay announced lunch was ready, they decided to call a time-out.

Luke, who ate more than his share of fast food due in part to his work schedule, always looked forward to one of Kay's spreads. She went all out again, so he loaded his plate from a smorgasbord of salads.

Danny, meanwhile, filled up on hot dogs, chips and soda. As a doctor who knew the value of good nutrition, Luke probably should say something, but since he didn't always practice what he preached, it seemed hypocritical to do it now.

"This is really cool," Danny said between mouthfuls. "My mom doesn't like me to have junk food, so I'm going to eat as much as I can while I have the chance."

Apparently, Leilani was more health conscious than Luke had realized. He hoped he wasn't going to regret this. *But heck, the kid deserved a little fun. Why squawk about it on their first day together as father and son?*

Before long, the boys started urging the men back on the grass for another round of Ultimate, but there hadn't been any arms that needed twisting, so the game began anew.

Luke wasn't sure how much time had passed when Nick said, "Hailey and I are going to have to call it a day. I've got to go into the precinct this evening."

"We've got to go, too," Joe said. "Bobby has a Boy Scout meeting to attend, so since the score is tied, the team that makes the next point wins."

As Luke put the disc into play, it was snatched by Bobby Davenport. Time was running out, so he was forced to get rid of it.

"I'm open," Danny yelled, as he broke free, running lickety-split.

Several of the other men had commented on his agility and speed, and Luke couldn't help but grin.

"Like father, like son," he'd quipped.

In a rush, Bobby sent the disc flying off to the side. And Danny, determined to catch it, ran as fast as he could.

"Just let it go," Luke said. "It's out of bounds."

Whether Danny didn't care or couldn't hear, it was tough to say.

As he neared the water fountain, running at top speed, Luke went on high alert. "Watch out!"

The boy glanced first at Luke, but by the time he turned his head toward the fountain, his feet couldn't keep up with the speed of his forward motion, and he tripped. The momentum sent him flying, and he landed with a thud, collapsing at the base of the concrete structure.

Damn. That was a hard fall. Luke started toward him, expecting the boy to get up crying. He wouldn't have blamed him.

But Danny didn't make a sound. Nor did he get up.

He just lay there, as still and silent as Kami had been.

Luke was at his side in a moment, and when he saw the gash on his head and the bright red flow of blood, he damn near forgot all his training.

For a moment, he saw Kami lying in a pool of blood in the street, still and unmoving. But he shook off the staggering memory, refusing to believe Danny's injury could be that serious.

Head wounds bled a lot and could be scary to the average person.

"Is he all right?" Nick asked, as the rest of the men and boys quickly gathered around.

"He's unconscious." Luke checked his head, probed his wound and made a trained assessment of his injuries.

"Should I call an ambulance?" Harry asked, as he pulled his cell phone out of his pocket.

"Yes." Luke figured it was for the best. He couldn't watch over him and drive at the same time.

And if anything unexpected went wrong, the ambulance would be better prepared for an emergency.

Damn. Leilani was going to be sick with worry.

And spitting mad. She'd think this was all Luke's fault, and he couldn't help thinking she'd be right.

He tried to focus on his medical skills, but seeing his own child in pain and injured tied him in a knot and made it tough to think.

Hell. He never cracked under pressure. *Never.* But right now, he felt more like Danny's father than a competent M.D.

When Danny moaned, coming to, Luke let out the breath he'd been holding. "Hey, buddy. How're you doing?"

The boy grimaced. "Ow. It hurts really bad."

"What hurts?"

"My head. My arm."

Luke glanced down at the boy's wrist. Aw, man. It didn't take an X-ray to diagnose this fracture. He looked into Danny's eyes. *Pupils seemed to be reacting fine.*

Nothing too serious. A mild concussion, a few stitches and a cast.

Damn. How was he going to tell Leilani? And why did this have to happen on his watch?

Kay hurried over with a clean cloth, while Caitlin Tanner, a nurse who sometimes worked with Luke at Oceana, brought a first aid kit and an ice pack.

"Need some help?"

Yeah. Help in telling Leilani.

"His mother is going to kill me," Luke muttered.

"Hey," Harry said. "It was an accident. Things like this happen."

Harry was right, of course. But Luke had promised to look after Danny, just as he had with Kami.

"Good thing he was going to the right, and not out in the parking lot," one of the boys said. "He could have been run over by a car. And that would have been worse."

Luke blinked back thoughts of Kami, and tried to shake off Leilani's possible reaction. Still, guilt and feelings of negligence damn near strangled him.

As a siren sounded in the distance, Danny reached for Luke's arm. "Do I have to go to the hospital?"

"Just for an hour or so." Five was more like it, although Luke had some pull. "You're going to need a few stitches, Danny." *At least ten.* "And you're also going to get a cool cast that all your friends can sign."

Danny grimaced again, and tears welled in his eyes.

"Are you afraid?" Luke asked.

"A little. Are you going with me?"

"Every step of the way."

"It hurts, Dad."

A bittersweet knot formed in Luke's chest. It was the first time Danny had blessed him with the title of Dad. But an unfortunate accident had led him to do so. That and the absence of his mother.

Luke knew he shouldn't feel guilty. Hell, it could have happened to any one of the kids here.

"Do we have to tell Mom?" Danny asked.

"Yes. I'll give her a call."

He just wasn't sure when to do it.

Now?

Or after he made sure the boy was cleaned up and mended?

Either way, that call was going to be the toughest he'd ever had to make.

Chapter Twelve

Leilani had just merged onto Interstate 5 from the 405 on her way back to San Diego when her cell rang.

In her own car, she had a nifty place in the console where she liked to keep the phone when driving, but they were in Addie's white sedan today.

"Can you please hand me my purse?" she asked her aunt. "It's on the floor by your feet."

Addie had been cool to her all day, answering only when she had to, so it wasn't any surprise that she did as she was asked without comment.

Leilani reached into the pouch that held her cell, hoping she didn't lose the connection before answering. "Hello?"

"It's Luke."

"Hi. How is everything?"

"We had a great time at the park." He paused. "Where are you?"

She glanced at the sign over the freeway and gave him her best guess. "Laguna Hills. I'm probably an hour and a half away. Is something wrong?"

"Not really. Danny's fine. But I'm going to have to take him to the E.R. for a couple of stitches."

"Stitches?" Her voice rose an octave.

Luke didn't respond right away, but Addie gasped. "Oh, dear God. Has something happened to Danny?"

Over the line, a siren sounded in the background, and Leilani's heart crashed to her stomach. "Oh, no. What's that? Is it an ambulance?"

"It's just a precaution. In fact, it's more for your benefit than anything."

"What happened?" she asked, a rising panic causing her voice to shake.

"Danny's fine, Leilani. Don't worry. Here, I'll let you talk to him."

Moments later, Danny got on the line, unable to mask the distress in his voice. "Hi, Mom."

"Honey, are you really okay? What happened?"

"I was playing Ultimate and got hurt. That's all."

"What kind of game is that?"

"It's a lot like football."

Leilani's stomach, which still seemed to house her pounding heart, twisted. And her hands, one holding the cell and the other on the wheel, tightened their grips until her knuckles ached.

"I gotta go now," he said. "Can I talk to you later? My arm really hurts."

"Your arm?"

"Yeah. Luke, I mean my dad, said it's broken and I'm going to have to wear a cast."

Bile rose in her throat. Stitches? A broken bone?

The siren grew louder. *For God's sake, Danny was going to the hospital in an ambulance.*

"I love you, baby. And I'll be there as quick as I can. Put your father on the line." When Luke's voice sounded, Leilani exploded. "Why on earth did you let him play football? You knew how I felt about that. And you promised to look out for him. But apparently your word doesn't mean anything."

Luke paused, as though pondering her accusation, then ignored it. "A football wasn't even involved. He was playing with a Frisbee. And for the record, Ultimate is a non-contact sport."

"Oh yeah? Then why is my son being transported to the hospital in an ambulance? It sounds awfully rough to me."

Addie shrieked. "I knew something like this would happen!"

Ignoring her aunt, Leilani continued to vent her disapproval. "How could you be so negligent? I trusted you to look out for him."

"I'm sorry," Luke said. "For what it's worth, his injury isn't serious."

After hanging up, Leilani shot a glance at Addie, who was pumped and ready to blow.

"Don't say it," Leilani snapped. "Your I-told-you-so is already repeating like a broken record in my brain."

Leilani doubted Addie would remain silent on the subject on the rest of the drive to San Diego, but maybe she'd keep quiet until they got a couple of miles down the road.

Pressing her foot down on the gas pedal, Leilani increased her speed beyond the posted limit, determined to get to the hospital as soon as she could.

She had to get to her son.

Luke had ridden with Danny in the ambulance, instructing them to take him to Oceana General, even though there was a closer hospital in Bayside. Along the way he'd taken vitals and further convinced himself the boy's injuries weren't serious. Of course, he doubted Leilani would see it that way.

He'd been careful to downplay the news about Danny getting hurt, but she'd still flipped.

I trusted you to look out for him.

Apparently your word doesn't mean anything.

How could you be so negligent?

Her accusations had lanced him to the bone. He'd tried to tell himself she was sick with worry, that she was responding with her heart and not her head. But clearly there was more going on than that.

After Kami died, Luke had tried to approach Leilani and her family to tell them his side of the story, to try and explain how it had come to happen, to apologize. But Leilani had refused to listen.

And he'd failed to reach her.

Now he suspected her unresolved anger over Kami's death colored her words and her reaction, which meant there wasn't a damn thing Luke could do about that.

Give him a textbook, a classroom or a clinical setting and he was a whiz. But throw him in an emotional quagmire and he was sunk.

After all, he'd even failed his mother in her time of need.

So what made him think he was any better at facing emotions head-on now?

He scanned the relatively empty waiting room, hoping to get his son treated as soon as possible. Since they'd arrived in an ambulance, they had priority. Before Luke could punch in the code to enter the exam rooms, Marge beat him to it.

"This is a surprise. The call came in about a laceration and fracture, but I didn't realize *you* were riding shotgun."

Luke nodded toward Danny. "This is my son."

His words seemed to give Marge pause, but she quickly stepped into unflappable-nurse mode and smiled at the boy. "It's nice to meet you, honey. What's your name?"

"Danny Stephens."

The last name is Wynter, Luke wanted to correct, but he let it go. "Do you have an empty bed for us?

I've got to get him cleaned up and looking present-able before his mother sees him."

"What can I do to help?"

"Have someone come in here and manually fill out the paperwork for me. I don't want to take time to wait while Esther inputs the information into the computer. Then get Stan Priestly, if he's on duty. Otherwise, I'll take whatever plastic surgeon we have available." Luke didn't expect the wound to scar badly, but he wasn't taking any chance of setting Leilani off further.

"Will do," Marge said, showing off her ability to take orders and reminding Luke why he liked working with her so much. "First of all, bed seven is empty. Consider it assigned to Danny. Dr. Priestly *is* somewhere in the building, so I'll have him paged. And I'll ask the new LVN to make sure we get Danny in the computer system."

He nodded, then escorted the paramedics to the vacant bed, realizing he'd neglected to thank Marge. But surely she knew her own value and how compe-tent he thought she was.

When the men had removed Danny from their gurney and had him settled, Luke shook their hands. He knew the various paramedics who routinely brought victims to Oceana, but Bayside was serviced by another hospital and fire department, so this was the first time he'd worked with these two. "Thanks."

"No problem, Doc."

As the paramedics left, Marge returned and pulled

the pale-green curtain providing limited privacy. It had never bothered Luke before, but he didn't want the entire floor to hear every damn thing that might transpire between him and Leilani, especially if she dragged her pinch-nosed aunt in here.

He wondered if he could come up with a way to keep Addie at a distance.

"How's it going?" Marge asked the boy.

"Okay. It hurts, though."

"What happened?" she asked.

"He had a collision with a water fountain at the park," Luke said.

"Looks like the fountain won the first round."

Not if Luke could help it. "We're going to need X-rays and a pediatric orthopedic specialist."

"I'll take care of it." Marge reached for the phone. After making the call, she stepped over to the sink and washed her hands. Then she slipped on a pair of gloves. "Let's see if we can get your face washed up a bit. I won't get anywhere near your wound."

Moments later, the LVN came in with the paperwork. Her badge said her name was Tatiana.

"Have a seat," Luke said. "And if you read off those questions, I'll answer them.

When she'd covered the basics, Tatiana asked, "Who's the responsible party?"

She was talking about financial responsibility, but Luke's thoughts went beyond the simple "I am" answer he gave her. *It's my fault. I never should have tried to talk his mother into letting him go to the park with me.*

Dammit. No matter how you looked at it, Luke wasn't to blame. But since Leilani seemed to think so, he couldn't help feeling guilty anyway, which made him want to throw up his hands, say "Screw it," and walk away.

He wouldn't though.

"Insurance?" Tatiana asked.

"He's not on my plan yet, so I'll pay in cash."

"Luke?" Harry's voice sounded from the doorway. "Are you in here?"

Luke turned and peered around the curtain. A sense of calm settled over him—not that he'd been shaky before, but the whole guilt thing had him uneasy. So just seeing Kay and Harry was a relief. "Hey, come on in."

The retired detective and his wife pulled the curtain back so they could come closer.

"Zack and Diana are here, too," Harry said. "They sent the girls home with the Tanners and wanted you to know they're available to run errands or whatever."

"I really appreciate that."

And he *did*, which was weird.

In the past, in cases where the patient's illness or injury was minor, like Danny's, Luke couldn't understand why a group of friends or family members would hang out in the waiting room. He'd usually get annoyed to see them taking up seats they didn't need.

In fact, several months ago, on a Saturday night, a drunken mother-of-the-bride had turned the ER into a zoo.

She'd started drinking champagne long before the ceremony, and by the time the reception began, she was three sheets to the wind. When the music started, she ran out to the dance floor in a pair of brand-new high heels, only to skid across the floor and fall, lacerating her hand on a shattered flute and breaking her foot as well.

An ambulance was called, and she was transported to the hospital. But then, the whole damn wedding party followed. Someone made a beer run, and the reception was continued in the waiting room until Marge had chased them out to the parking lot, where the party resumed.

That was definitely too much.

But this? No comparison.

"Tell Zack and Diana that I appreciate their support." Interestingly enough, Luke-the-doctor and Luke-the-dad seemed to be two entirely different beings.

And Luke-the-dad was off stride. The fact that his friends had rallied touched him in an unexpected way. Their support, he realized, would also come in handy. When Leilani arrived, he was going to need someone in his corner, witnesses who could convince her that he hadn't been negligent. That this accident could have happened on her watch.

Of course, if she *would* have been there, she probably would have made the poor kid sit on the sidelines.

Kay, who'd been holding Danny's backpack by

one of the straps, lifted it, showing it to Luke. "We weren't sure if you'd need this or not."

Luke eyed the bag Leilani had insisted they take— just in case. "Thanks, Kay. That might come in handy. See if he has a different shirt in there."

Kay unzipped the bag, then rummaged through it. "You're in luck. And we've got pants, too."

"Good. When his mother arrives, I want him in clean clothes."

Kay whipped out the shirt and pants. "I'll step out while you help him change, and when you're done, I'll take the soiled garments home. I'm good at getting stains out."

Luke's first thought was to tell her to throw away the bloody garments as if he'd committed a crime and was trying to get rid of evidence. But ten stitches and a cast was incriminating enough.

"Thanks. You're a sweetheart." He gave Kay the hug he'd felt compelled to give earlier. "And since I suspect you have more pull with The Big Guy upstairs than most people, maybe you can ask for some divine help. I've never been good at emotional confrontations, and Danny's mother isn't at all happy with me."

Kay fingered the gold cross that hung from a delicate chain on her neck and smiled. "I'll see what I can do."

When they were alone, Luke helped the boy out of his shirt.

"Ow! Ooh. Ow."

"We'll get you something for the pain soon," Luke said.

"Is it a pill?" Danny asked. "I don't like the other kind of medicine. The pink stuff makes me puke."

"Actually, it's an injection. It works better and faster."

Danny scrunched his face. "You mean a shot? Those hurt."

"Nah. It shouldn't even faze a guy like you. Most kids your age would have been screaming and crying after a collision like that, but you're tough."

"Yeah, well, there were girls there, too. And you know how it is."

Luke knew Danny was talking about Zack and Diana's daughters and smiled. "Girls can sure put a guy in an awkward position sometimes."

While Danny seemed to ponder that idea, Luke stroked his shoulder. "I'll make sure we find the very best shot-giver in the hospital."

Before Danny could respond, the plastic surgeon arrived. Luke greeted Stan Priestly, then stepped aside as the physician checked Danny's wound.

When the needle was inserted to numb the wound, Luke held his son's hand, felt the desperate squeeze of his fingers and watched him grimace in pain. Yet the boy was as quiet as a courageous mouse.

"You know," Luke said, "I'm glad you're brave and tough. But it's okay to cry out if it really hurts."

"It wasn't that bad."

Ten minutes later, the wound had been flushed and the edges trimmed for a clean suture. If Luke's luck held, Danny would be back from his X-ray and wearing a cast before his mother arrived.

Maybe she would calm down on the ride here.

She sure hadn't taken the news very well. And with Addie in the car and undoubtedly coming to the hospital with her, he figured all hell could break loose when they walked through the door.

Unless Kay's prayers worked.

While they waited for Dr. Erickson, who ought to be coming in anytime, Luke couldn't help listening to the conversation taking place on the other side of the curtain.

"Howard," an older woman admonished, "if I've told you once, I've told you a thousand times. You have no business climbing on ladders."

"I'm not an invalid," an elderly male said, the frailty in his voice belying his words. "The day I can't take care of myself or my place, is the day I lay down and die."

"Well, you nearly did that today. You're eighty-three years old, Howard. And you're lucky you only banged up your face and your shoulder. You could have broken your neck. Or a hip, for goodness' sake. And then where would you be?"

The only response was a moan.

"And *now* look at you," the woman continued. "If you would have waited just five minutes, I would have called a repairman to adjust the antenna, but oh, no. You had to climb on that roof and fix it yourself."

Another moan tore through the silence, this one

longer and more drawn out. Maybe Howard had done more than bang up his face and shoulder.

When the LVN who'd helped Luke get the paperwork completed returned with Danny's ID bracelet, the man's wife called her to bed eight. "Where is the doctor? My husband is in pain."

"Dr. Freidman will be here shortly. I think you're up next."

Luke usually was so busy on his shifts that he rarely paid much attention to the chatter. But as a father who was waiting with his son, it was easy to get sucked in and to connect with the individuals and their pain. He sympathized with the man who'd wanted to maintain his dignity and make a simple repair he'd probably done a hundred times over the years, a job his aging body wasn't up to anymore.

The patient in bed six had been riding a quad and was involved in an off-road accident. As Brad Tillman, another of Luke's colleagues, told the parents that their daughter would need an MRI to rule out any internal bleeding, they'd remained calm. But when the girl had been wheeled out, they collapsed in a tearful embrace.

Luke could relate to the couple trying to be strong in front of their child. Aware of the complications that could occur, they had to be worried sick. Thank goodness Danny's head injury hadn't been serious.

Upon Brad's return, he asked the parents if they had any questions for him, questions they hadn't wanted to voice when their daughter was present.

Then he took a chair beside them, his voice gentle yet competent. He addressed their fears and concerns as if their daughter was his only patient that night.

It's not as though Luke was a brash or cocky doctor, he just held his emotions in check. But that didn't mean he wasn't always up-front and honest with people. He answered questions and offered possible options, too. It's just that he didn't get any more involved than that; he couldn't afford to.

As he watched the parents nod, their expressions shedding the fear and distress they'd held moments before, he was forced to reconsider his own brisk bedside manner. He supposed it could be improved upon. At least, a little.

"Dr. Wynter?" Marge asked, as she poked her head around the curtain.

"Yes?"

"If Danny's mother is the pretty brunette who was so worried about Carrie Summers and has been visiting the ICU regularly, she just arrived."

Uh-oh. Luke had a feeling another E.R. drama was about to unfold in the waiting room.

Only this time, he'd be in the thick of it.

By the time Leilani arrived at the hospital, she was beside herself with worry, anger and frustration. Luke had said Danny was all right and the injury was minor, but she needed to see him and come to that conclusion herself.

On top of feeling concern for her son, she was mad

at Luke for putting Danny at risk. Then she'd had to listen to Addie vent for miles about delinquency, drug use and premarital sex. And as if that weren't enough, her aunt had segued into family betrayal and how difficult it was to regain someone's trust.

Leilani had wanted to say something in her defense, but she hadn't. What good would it have done? Addie could be stubborn at times, and this was one of them.

Now Leilani and Addie entered the ER at Oceana General and scanned the waiting room, looking for a registration desk of some kind. Leilani needed to ask someone to take her to Danny's bedside immediately.

Spotting a woman who appeared to be a reception-ist behind a glass window, Leilani started toward her, only to have Kay Logan intercept her with a smile and a hug. "Danny's doing fine, Leilani."

"Where is he?"

"The last I heard, he was back in an exam room. But he could be in X-ray by now. Luke said he has a broken arm."

Leilani blew out a ragged breath, ready to unload on the kindhearted woman, but knew that wasn't fair.

"It's always tough when children get hurt," Kay said. "I had three boys and hate to say it, but broken bones and stitches ought to be added to the childhood ditty about snips, snails and puppy dog tails."

Leilani knew boys tended to play rough. That's why she tried to monitor Danny's games and ac-tivities. And that's why she'd asked Luke not to let Danny play football.

Okay, so they weren't exactly playing football, but he knew why she'd made the request and should have respected her wishes. And if in doubt, he could have called her. Yet he'd let her down—*again.*

"I know I'm protective of Danny," Leilani admitted, "but I feel as though I have to be. Danny is all I have."

Other than Addie, of course, and her grandfather in Hawaii.

To be honest, Leilani was angry at both Luke and Addie.

For the past hour, Leilani had listened to a barrage of complaints about Luke's character and even though a part of her had wanted to agree, Addie hadn't needed any extra ammo with which to assault him with a snarl or a snide comment. Luke was still Danny's father, so Leilani had clamped her mouth shut for so long that her jaw ached.

"Luke feels badly about this," Kay said.

"He ought to. I was reluctant to even let Danny go to the park without me, but Luke promised he'd watch out for him."

Before Kay could respond, Luke—speak of the devil—strode out of the exam area and entered the waiting room, looking dashing and sheepish at the same time. How could she want to embrace him yet want to shake the stuffing out of him, too?

She cursed her weakness for him, as well as the dark cloud that seemed to follow him whenever he was with someone she loved.

"Come on," he said, placing a hand on her arm. "I'll take you back to see Danny."

As Addie began to follow, Luke stopped her. "I'm sorry, Mrs. Stephens. We're cramped back there right now, and hospital regulations won't allow more than one person in the room with him."

Addie let out a "humph" and crossed her arms, but she stayed behind.

Leilani wondered if Luke could pull strings and get her aunt back there, but she wouldn't make an issue out of it. Actually, she could use a break from Addie.

Luke escorted Leilani to bed seven, where Danny sat up, cradling his arm.

"Are you okay, baby?" she asked.

"Yeah. See my stitches?"

How could she not? They were splayed along the left side of his forehead, near the eyebrow. He almost seemed proud of them.

"Too bad it's not Halloween yet," Danny said. "I could be Frankenstein, huh?"

"A plastic surgeon stitched him up," Luke said. "There shouldn't be much of a scar."

Leilani refused to even think about that.

"I'm going to get a cast, too," Danny added, as though he'd gone through some rite of passage while she'd been gone. "And you can be the first one to sign it."

She forced a smile, but before she could conjure a response, the curtain was pulled back, and a physician stepped in.

"I'm Dr. Erickson." He greeted Leilani and Danny, then patted Luke on the back. "I hear you're responsible for this." The silver-haired man chuckled, but Leilani didn't find anything humorous about what he apparently considered a joke.

A scowl on Luke's face suggested he hadn't found it funny, either.

As Dr. Erickson examined Danny's arm, he agreed with the preliminary diagnosis. "It's broken, but I'll need to see the X-ray."

He placed the order, then called one of the hospital orderlies to take Danny to radiology.

"Cool," Danny said. "I never got to ride in a wheelchair before."

"It's not necessary for you to go with him," Dr. Erickson told Leilani and Luke. "We'll let you both know when he's on his way back, and you can be here waiting for him."

Leilani opened her mouth to object, but Danny grinned and said, "Cool. Tell Mom how tough I am, Dad."

Luke agreed. "He's a brave boy."

Yes, she supposed he was. But she'd noticed that her son had referred to Luke as his dad. Apparently, they were bonding already, which was probably great for the two of them, but unsettling for her.

Leilani brushed a kiss on Danny's brow, then watched the orderly wheel him away. As the mother of an injured child, she'd been worried for the past hour or so and wanted to lash out and tell Luke he could never see Danny again. But as a social worker she knew she couldn't keep him away forever. Nor would it be in Danny's best interest for her to try.

So rather than stand and gape at the boy who was growing up before her eyes or to risk raising her voice at his father, she decided to give Addie an update and headed for the waiting room.

Footsteps behind her suggested Luke was coming, too.

In spite of her resolve to be civil and calm, she couldn't help turning and letting a retort roll out of her mouth.

"I'm not going to let you take him anywhere again. Not unless I'm there to supervise."

Leilani's words stung Luke like salt on an abrasion. She had no idea how badly he felt about all of this, how hard he'd tried to go above and beyond the call of duty to ensure Danny was all right.

But it was clear to him what was happening.

As Leilani turned to the door, he took her by the arm, holding her back. "Listen, honey. It was an accident. Plain and simple."

She didn't say anything, but her response rang out loud and clear. *You're two for two. Kami's death had been an* accident, *too.*

Luke released his grip and crossed his arms. "I'm not going to apologize again. It's more than Danny's injury stirring you up. You still hold me responsible for your brother's death. And it's apparent you always will."

Her silence was all the evidence he needed. Whatever they'd shared—past or present—was over.

"I've put all that behind me," she said.

"No you haven't. And if you think you have, you're kidding yourself. You're going to be a bitter old woman someday, just like Addie."

Their gazes locked, and for a moment, they stood in some awkward time warp—their fragile relationship frayed at the seams.

"I don't want to talk about this now. Not here."

"All right," he said, taking back the pride he'd tossed at her feet. "But one more thing before you walk through those doors. Whether you like it or not, I'm going to be a part of Danny's life. I will, however, make every effort to stay out of yours."

Her eyes welled with unshed tears. Then she nodded and entered the waiting room, severing the final thread that held them together.

Luke blew out a dying sigh, then followed her so he could thank his friends and tell them he was leaving.

Addie, who'd been seated alone, quickly stood and strode to meet Leilani. "How's Danny? What's going on?"

"He's fine. Right now they're taking him to X-ray. Once he gets a cast, they'll let us take him home."

"Good." Addie shot a glare at Luke, who was several feet away, then took a seat next to Leilani by the door.

Wanting as much distance from the two women as he could get, Luke strode across the room and plopped down in an empty seat next to the Logans and the Hendersons.

"What's up?" Harry asked.

Luke leaned back, stretching his legs out in front of him and blowing out another sigh. On the outside, he appeared resigned, but on the inside he was dying.

Why hadn't she been able to let go of the past?

He'd never discussed the details of Kami's accident with anyone, not after talking to the police at the scene. And he'd never told anyone about the guilt that had dogged him nor mentioned the longing to go back in time and do things differently.

He'd always reasoned that was a conversation he needed to have with Leilani first, before sharing it with anyone else. But after tonight he might not ever have a chance to tell her, and he had to get it off his chest.

So he revealed it all, the accident, the blame, the shame.

His friends rallied around him, and like a dried-up old sponge, he soaked up their sympathy, their understanding.

Damn, it felt good. So he continued, catching them up to speed. "When Leilani came to the hospital with Carrie, it was the first time I'd seen her in twelve years. A couple of days later, I found out about Danny. She hadn't even bothered to tell me I had a son."

Kay placed her hand on his back, giving him a maternal caress that he'd been missing since long before his mother had taken her life. "Would you like me to talk to her, Luke?"

"What about?" Luke straightened in his seat and looked at Harry's wife. "She won't even let me explain how it all happened. And I'm not going to wallow in guilt for another twelve years. It might be easiest to walk away completely, which would undoubtedly make her happy, but I can't abandon my son. I know the effect something like that can have on a boy."

"Doing the right thing isn't always easy," Kay said.

"No it's not. But tap-dancing around my son's mother is going to be a pain in the ass."

When Kay didn't answer, Luke realized he should have watched his words as well as his tone.

Before he could apologize, Marge's voice stopped him. "Danny is on his way back from radiology, and Dr. Erickson would like to meet you in the exam room."

"Tell his mother," Luke said. Then on second thought, he added, "Please."

Marge cocked her head slightly, as though trying to sort it all out, then did as he requested.

Luke should get up and leave now, but he owed Danny an explanation of some kind, or at least a goodbye. So he went back to the exam room.

At Danny's bedside, Dr. Erickson showed Luke and Leilani the X-ray. "It's a clean break. We'll get it taken care of and send you on your way."

The doctor went on to explain to Danny that the shot would hurt a bit, then his arm would be numb and feel a whole lot better. "Before you know it, we'll have Humpty Dumpty together again."

Maybe so. But all the king's horses and all the king's men couldn't do a damn thing about putting Luke's family together again.

And it hurt something fierce.

How could a man miss something he'd scarcely known?

As Danny was given a choice of fiberglass colors for his cast, the hospital paging system announced, "Dr. Wynter, dial two-oh-one. Dr. Wynter, dial two-oh-one."

Damn. "And I thought this day couldn't get any worse." Luke hadn't realized he'd muttered the words until Danny addressed him.

"What's wrong, Dad?"

"It's a call from the ICU." Luke knew there was only one reason and one patient that would have initiated a page for him.

Leilani turned and reached for his arm, her eyes growing wide and concern temporarily washing the anger from her expression. "Could that have anything to do with Carrie?"

"Probably." There was only one way to find out.

He excused himself to answer the page.

Chapter Thirteen

"**I** know you're not on duty tonight," Bethany told Luke over the phone, "but I heard that you were in the hospital."

"You heard right." Luke gripped the receiver as he awaited the news. Losing Carrie right now would be a tough blow for Leilani, and as much as he'd told himself it was over between them, that he didn't give a rat's ass about her anymore, it wasn't true.

"Carrie came out of her coma," Bethany said. "She's asking about her baby and wants to see Leilani. I thought you'd want to know."

"Thanks. That's great news. How does she look? Does there seem to be any sign of brain damage?"

"None that's apparent. She's being examined by the neurologist right now, and they're running tests."

"I'll pass on the news."

"Carrie can't have visitors just yet," Bethany added. "And I have no idea how long the doctors will be with her. If Leilani wants to wait, she can probably see her later tonight."

"I understand."

When he'd disconnected the line, he went in search of Leilani and found her in the waiting room. Danny, who'd been released, stood at her side, examining a blue cast on his arm.

"I can't give you too many details," he told Leilani. "But Carrie is out of the coma and talking."

"Oh, thank God." Her shoulders slumped in relief.

In spite of all they'd been through today—the harsh words she'd said, the accusations—he felt compelled to slip an arm around her, to draw her near, to share her joy.

He wouldn't, of course.

"When can I see her?" she asked.

"It'll be a while yet." Luke crossed his arms, wanting that distance he'd been trying to create earlier.

"Will they let her see the baby tonight?" she asked, drawing him back into her world.

"That's a question for her doctor."

"I need to take Addie and Danny home," she said. "But I hate to leave until I've had a chance to see Carrie. I have a digital camera in my purse and I'd like to take some pictures of the baby so I can show them to her. She'll be eager to see him and know he's okay."

Diana, who'd been sitting quietly, stepped forward. "Please let Zack and I take your aunt and Danny home for you. We came by so that we could help out if needed."

"Thanks." A smile of relief broke out on her face. "I'd appreciate that." Then she turned to Addie. "Would you mind looking out for Danny tonight?"

"Of course not." The woman risked a look at Luke, and her eyes said, *Someone should take proper care of him.*

As Addie turned to get her handbag, Luke couldn't help the wry grin that tweaked his lips.

What would Addie do if she learned that Zack, a gentle hulk of a man, had spent five years in prison?

Of course, Zack had been convicted of a crime he hadn't committed, but he was a felon just the same.

Harry tapped Luke on the shoulder. "How about taking a walk outside?"

Since Luke decided Leilani didn't have need of him anymore, he agreed.

And he refused to glance over his shoulder for a final gaze at the woman who'd stomped on his heart.

Leilani had been through the proverbial wringer today, so she took a seat and let her emotions run free.

She had a lot to be thankful for. Danny's injury hadn't been all that serious. And since Carrie was asking about the baby, it was possible that she'd suffered only minor brain damage—if any at all. Yet something threatened to steal her joy.

A tear slipped down her cheek. And then another.

Before long, she sat weeping, and she couldn't even put her finger on why.

Kay took the seat beside her. "Are you okay, honey?"

Leilani wanted to say she was fine. Instead, she swiped at her tears and answered truthfully. "I don't get it. God allowed Carrie to pull through, which was a miracle, if you ask me, and an answer to prayer. But why was she spared when my brother wasn't?"

"I don't know why some people are taken and others are healed, but it helps if you remember that life is a journey. We're all just passing through, so we need to enjoy our friends and loved ones while they're here."

"That's easy for you to say," Leilani said. "You have a large, extended family."

"Yes, I do. I'm blessed and grateful, but I've suffered my losses, too."

Leilani glanced up, feeling a bit selfish for thinking she was the only one who'd ever been hurt. "I'm sorry to hear that."

"Harry and I had three sons," Kay said. "Steven, the oldest, was the most like me. I understood him, and we shared a closeness I didn't have with the other boys."

Leilani listened, realizing the older woman was talking in past tense.

"Steven had a strong sense of right and wrong, and even though I was opposed to him joining the military…" She turned to Leilani and placed a hand on her knee. "I'm as patriotic as anyone you'll ever meet, but I'm sure you'll understand my fear. I was afraid something might happen to him, that I might lose him."

Leilani didn't even want to think about Danny growing up and going to war.

"Steven fought in Desert Storm and, and three days before his tour of duty was up he died in a helicopter accident."

"I'm so sorry." Leilani took Kay's hand in hers. "I can't imagine your pain, your loss."

"Harry and I told ourselves that Steven had died in the line of duty, that he was a hero. A soldier. That he'd died for freedom." She cleared her throat. "But when we learned the details, we were beside ourselves with grief, anger, you name it."

"What do you mean? What happened?"

"Steven and the other men were in a Black Hawk, flying a routine mission, when they were blown out of the sky. But it wasn't the enemy who'd fired. One of our own men made a mistake, a miscalculation, and shot them down."

Leilani's stomach rolled, and tears welled up again. Words couldn't express her sympathy for Kay.

"The men on that helicopter were killed by what they call 'friendly fire,'" Kay said, turning and facing Leilani. "It would have been so easy to blame the government, the military or the poor soldier who'd been responsible. But anger and bitterness would have sucked us into an ugly trap, and we chose not to let it."

How could they not?

"To be honest," Kay said, "we did for a while. But then, during a moment of prayer, God spoke to me."

Leilani merely stared at her.

"It wasn't a conversation that you could have eavesdropped on, but I sensed His presence and His words. Steven's reasons for fighting had been noble, and the manner of his death hadn't lessened the value of his life, his valor or his honor."

Leilani thought it would be hard to let go and go on. But she didn't say anything.

"I was convinced that Steven was in Heaven and happier than I could imagine. I also realized that if I didn't find it in my heart to forgive and move forward, the anger and resentment would have eventually crippled me and everyone around me."

Leilani didn't know what to say.

Kay smiled. "Let me share something with you that Mark Twain once said."

"What's that?"

"Forgiveness is the fragrance the violet sheds on the heel that crushed it."

It was a pretty sentiment and visual.

"Perhaps you've noticed the breakfast nook in my kitchen. It's a reminder of a choice I made and the life I wanted to live." Kay stood, then cupped Leilani's cheek. "I'll let you think on that for a while."

As Kay turned and walked away, that's exactly what Leilani did.

She'd been to the Logans' house the day of the

brunch and had entered the kitchen, where she'd sat at the oak table in the small sitting room. A big bay window was adorned by white lace curtains. Lavender walls were trimmed with a strip of wallpaper, something feminine and pretty. A flower print, if Leilani recalled.

Violets.

In the corner, a plant stand with white shelves held a variety of potted flowers—all of them violets.

Kay's decor had a theme, a subtle reminder to forgive those who'd trespassed against her.

The moment Kay had invited her inside, Leilani had sensed something special about the house, something warm and peaceful. At the time, Leilani had been amazed at how the home in which she now stayed paled in comparison. But not because Addie's furniture was worn or because the apartment building was old.

The furnishings of the Goldmans, who lived in the same complex, had seen a lot of use, too, yet a cozy aura had blessed their home in the same way it did Kay's.

Ruth Goldman was raising her grandson. Leilani didn't know why, but she suspected the reason had something to do with a parent's death, desertion or drug addiction—any of which could make a person sad or bitter. Yet like Kay, the Goldmans chose not to be.

Something Luke said came to mind. *You're going to be a bitter old woman someday, just like Addie.*

Leilani had wanted to object, to tell him that he didn't know the real Addie, who'd been a loving

aunt over the years and had always been supportive and kind.

That was true, but Addie had also held a grudge
against Uncle Bob. When they'd been married thirty-
two years, Bob had suffered some kind of midlife
crisis. He left home for six months to find himself,
and when he returned, Addie refused to take him
back. He came to her several times after that, hoping
to reconcile, but she refused, saying his abandonment
had hurt and embarrassed her.

"I'll never forgive him," Addie had said more than
once. And she'd said the same thing about Luke.

Now Leilani suspected Addie would hold that
same attitude toward her no matter how many times
she apologized.

Apparently, there was a pattern there, and it ran
deep. Leilani recalled the story Addie had told about
being an errant but penitent child.

No, Addie's father had told her, *I will* not *accept
your apology, because you should have never done
it in the first place.*

What a terrible thing for a child to hear; what an
awful way to grow up.

Anger and bitterness ate away at the unforgiving
person. And worse, the self-destructive attitude
seemed to pass from parent to child.

Addie had raised Leilani's father when he'd been
orphaned as a boy, yet when it came to draw up their
will, Leilani's parents had requested her maternal
grandparents have custody of the children if anything

happened to them. Addie had been crushed to learn she'd been bypassed.

Now Leilani suspected she knew the reason why her parents had made their wishes clear. They'd wanted their children to grow up in a loving home, where they would learn to forgive.

After Kami died, Leilani had almost forgotten everything her parents had valued.

When Luke had come by to talk to her, she'd refused to see him. And when he'd later called, hoping to explain what had happened, she'd hung up on him, thinking there was no excuse for what he'd done.

Just recently, he'd tried to explain again, but she'd shut him out, intent on holding the remnants of her little family together.

Imitating Addie.

Creating a home of bitterness and intolerance.

Now it was time to break the cycle, even if approaching Luke now was too little, too late.

After drying her tears, Leilani went into the NICU, where baby Michael lay sleeping. She caught several darling shots of him, then took the camera up to the ICU, hoping she would be allowed to see Carrie soon.

"You can come in," a redheaded nurse said, "but just for a few minutes."

Leilani made her way to her friend's bedside and took her hand. "Hey, Carrie. How are you?"

Carrie opened her eyes and gave Leilani's hand a

weak squeeze. "I'm okay, but how is the baby? They told me he was doing fine, but they won't let me see him yet. Maybe tomorrow."

"Well, I have the next best thing." Leilani whipped out her camera and brought up Michael's picture. "Look at this little guy."

Carrie opened her eyes and studied the beautiful baby she had yet to meet. "Oh my goodness. He's precious. Isn't he?"

"He's beautiful," Leilani said, "and a real sweetheart. I've been visiting him often, and I've told him all about you."

Carrie smiled, eyes closing, as though trying to preserve her strength.

"Listen, Carrie. I'm going to let you sleep. I'll see you in the morning, okay?"

"Uh-huh."

As Leilani left the ICU, she whispered a prayer of thanksgiving, then headed to the parking lot. She had one more stop to make.

It was getting late, so there weren't many cars on the road, and the drive to Bayside went quickly. The moon, like her heart, was full yet obscured by a cloud.

As she turned into Playa del Sol, her heart heavy, she continued on until she found a visitor's parking space. Her first impulse had been to check the mirror, to run a brush through her hair, to add a dab of lipstick, but she was coming here to apologize to Luke, and it seemed only fitting that she be humble about it.

She slipped her arm through the shoulder strap

of her purse, then headed for the door of Luke's condo. The porch light was off, but a blue-tinted glow in the living room window suggested he was watching television.

She knocked and, for a moment, wondered whether he'd fallen asleep and hadn't heard her. Then the knob turned and the door slowly opened.

He stood before her, shirtless, his hair tousled. He wore a pair of sweatpants, low on his hips. And she found her pulse skittering, skipping. Strumming.

"Can I come in?" she asked. "Please?"

He stepped aside. "Is Carrie doing all right?"

"Yes. I showed her a photo of the baby and promised to see her again tomorrow. She was pretty tired." She smoothed imaginary wrinkles from her slacks, then scanned the room. "Do you mind if I sit?"

"Go ahead." He flicked on the lamp, then strode to the coffee table, picked up the remote and turned down the volume of an action flick he'd been watching.

She took a seat on the edge of the sofa. "I came to apologize to you."

"No need to."

"Yes, there is. I was wrong to lash out at you. And I behaved as badly and rudely as Addie. There's no excuse for it, and I hope you'll forgive me."

He shrugged, yet didn't appear to soften any. "You were worried about Danny. I realize that."

"Yes, but I should have been more understanding. Accidents happen. I'm sorry for my outburst, as well

as my distrust. You can take him again, and I don't
need to be present."

"All right."

"I'm also sorry for not contacting you when I first
learned that I was pregnant." She paused, allowing
him time to forgive her, to say something, but he
remained standing. As rigid as she'd been to him.

He wasn't making this easy for her, but she
couldn't blame him. After all, he'd tried to explain
and apologize to her many times, and she'd refused
to hear him out.

Every time she thought about Kami's accident,
she was sucked into a whirlpool of grief, and it had
been easier to avoid thinking about it, avoid talking
about it. She'd counseled people who used that same
defensive strategy, so why she hadn't taken her own
advice was beyond her.

"I also want to tell you that I forgive you for taking
Kami to that party," she added. "And I apologize for
not allowing you to tell your side of the story."

Something began to thaw in his eyes, so she
continued.

"It's always been tough for me to think about
Kami's death, so I've refused to talk about it to anyone.
And somehow, because I'd tried not to dwell on it, I
told myself that I'd put it behind me. But that's not the
same as addressing the issue and moving on. So if
you're willing to discuss it now, I'm ready to listen."

Luke uncrossed his arms, then took a seat on the
sofa. Not too close, yet not too far.

"When you left for that college tour," he began, "you asked me to look out for Kami. Later that night, I saw him at the market. Addie had asked him to pick up some eggs."

The accident had happened on Saturday, so she wasn't sure why he was giving her a play-by-play, but she would listen and allow him to continue at his own pace.

"I asked if he wanted to go have an ice cream or something, but he said he couldn't. He suggested we go the next night, when Addie would be playing cards with some friends."

Even Kami had to sneak around in order to see Luke. Not that it was right, but sometimes adults were so strict that they encouraged kids to be sly.

Oh, God. Was Leilani too strict with Danny? Was she putting him in a position where deceit might seem to be his only option?

Luke leaned back in his seat, stretching an arm across the backrest. "The next morning, a couple of buddies told me about a party they were going to attend that evening. I told them I couldn't make it, but they started hounding me again about not having time for them. So I said I'd stop by for a while, planning to make a showing."

Leilani had never liked his friends. Several times, when she'd been with him, their teasing had bordered on harassment.

"On Saturday night, I met Kami in front of the Eberly Arms, then headed to the diner for a hot fudge sundae. Afterward, I walked him home. We said goodbye, but when I reached the house where the party was being held, I heard footsteps and turned."

"He followed you?"

"Yes. My first thought was to send him home, but he said it was boring at Addie's, and I felt sorry for him. I figured I'd go inside, say hi to a few people so they'd know I was there, then cut out and spend the rest of the evening with him. Maybe see a movie or something."

Leilani continued to listen, to let Luke explain.

"We hadn't been there long, maybe twenty minutes or so, when a couple of drug dealers showed up. So I decided to cut out, but I couldn't find Kami. Someone said he'd gone upstairs, so I searched there." Luke raked a hand through his hair. "When I came back to the living room, it was jammed with bodies and filled with loud music. I thought Kami might have gotten uncomfortable and walked home, and that scared me."

"Why?"

"Kami had been sheltered and protected his whole life, and I knew he could get into big trouble on the city streets. So I shoved myself through the crowd and went outside, where I found him holding a can of soda and talking to a couple of guys."

"Who were they?" she asked.

"I don't know. I'd never seen them before. The three of them were laughing, but there was something wrong with Kami. His eyes were glassy, and he was fidgety."

Luke paused, allowing himself to relive that tragic evening. The very moment things went from bad to worse. "I grabbed the can out of Kami's hand, and he tried to take it back. His words were slurred, and he swore at me, something he'd never done. I told him you were going to skin me alive if I didn't take him home, but he didn't care."

"His soda had been spiked," Leilani said. "The autopsy revealed he'd been high on PCP."

Luke nodded. "His attitude and behavior, as well as the crazed look in his eye, told me it was more than booze."

"Where did he get it?" she asked.

"I have no idea who gave it to him, and if I hadn't been in a hurry to get him out of there, I would have tried to find out. I'd never felt responsible for anyone other than myself, and the urge to protect Kami was overwhelming."

"Then what happened?" Leilani asked.

"A siren sounded in the distance, and I reached for the sleeve of Kami's shirt. 'Come on,' I told him. 'We've got to go, dude. *Now*.'" Luke turned to Leilani, his eyes beseeching her to understand. "Usually he jumped to do whatever I suggested, but not that night. Instead he flipped out, jerked away and dashed into the street, right in front of the speeding car. The driver, one of the drug dealers who'd been inside, didn't even stop."

Luke's mind took him back, the vision as clear tonight as it had been back then. But he wouldn't share the gory details. He'd rushed to the street, where Kami lay in a pool of blood. His body mangled and still.

In health class, Luke had learned CPR, so he tried to save Kami's life, but to no avail.

"At least the police caught them," Leilani said.

"They cut off the drug dealer's car as it sped away. And I continued CPR until the paramedic arrived."

His words sounded so clinical, almost like a newspaper account, but it had been so much worse than that.

"Don't die," he'd begged the boy with each compression of his chest. "Please, don't die."

But all the pleading in the world hadn't done one damn bit of good. Kami *had* died. And the blood on Luke's hands was a reminder of his failure to do the right thing.

Luke turned to Leilani. "I tried to help him, but it was too late. A couple of years later, I talked to one of the paramedics who'd been there that night. He said Kami had died upon impact, but they didn't stop working on him until he was pronounced at the hospital."

There. It was out.

All he could do was wait, as Leilani sat there, taking it all in.

Then she reached for his hand, her fingers threading through his. "It wasn't your fault, Luke. Kami should have stayed home. He knew better than to follow you."

"Yeah, but I shouldn't have let him step one foot inside that party, and for that I'll never forgive myself."

Leilani tugged at his hand, pulling him toward her. Her eyes met his. "There's nothing to forgive. You were a kid. You made a choice that, under normal circumstances, wouldn't have been wrong. It was the drug that made Kami run in front of the car."

"I tried to find out who did it, who slipped him the PCP in his drink, but I never did. And I suppose that was a good thing. I would have put the bastard in the hospital or worse."

"Then I'm glad you didn't find out. That might have ruined your life." Her hand lifted, her fingers touched his cheek, brushed against the light stubble he would shave in the morning. "Do you think we can start over and put the past behind us now?"

He placed his hand over the top of hers, claiming her touch, reinforcing a connection he hoped would last a lifetime. "There's nothing I'd like better, Lani."

She grinned. "I'd always told you to call me Lani, but you rarely did."

"In the past, I figured it was a nickname reserved for family, and I was always on the outside looking in."

"Not anymore. You're the father of my son. And the only man I've ever loved."

Luke's heart soared. "I've never stopped loving you, either, honey." Then he pulled her into his arms and kissed her.

And when he released her, he took her hand and led her into his bedroom, where they made love, celebrating the journey they were about to embark upon. The love they shared, the life they wanted for themselves and their son.

A life filled with love and second chances.

Epilogue

The day Luke and Leilani would become man and wife shined as sunny and bright as their future promised to be.

Kay and Harry Logan hosted the small wedding in their backyard, like they had for several other young couples in Bayside. The parklike grounds, dotted with the white rental chairs and a gazebo adorned with flowers, looked lovely today. Fairy tale perfect.

In Kay's guest room, Leilani took one last look in the mirror and checked the tiny violets the hairdresser had tucked along the edge of her veil. It was nearly time to start.

When a knock sounded, she turned to see Addie enter. Their relationship was still somewhat strained, but after Addie had received a surprise visit from Kay, she'd reluctantly agreed to give Luke and Leilani a chance.

"Well, now," Addie said. "Don't you look pretty."

"Thank you."

"I brought you something." Her aunt lifted the brown paper sack she held.

"What is it?"

"Just a little something I picked up. Got one for myself, too, but left it in the car. Hope it doesn't get too hot out there."

Leilani peeked into the bag, spotted a violet in a pot, and grinned. The words might not have been spoken, but she heard the message loud and clear. Addie was going to try and forgive them both.

"Thank you, Addie. I love you. And this gift is going to get a place of honor in our home."

It had been decided that they would live in Luke's condo, which Leilani had already begun to decorate. The movers had brought her things south, and she'd managed to create a warm, cozy place they all would enjoy coming home to.

Another knock sounded, and this time Carrie entered the room with baby Michael in her arms. "Kay said I should ask if you were ready. Obviously, you are. You look absolutely beautiful. And your smile is dazzling."

"I've never been happier," Leilani said.

"Where will you be going on your honeymoon?"

"To Hawaii. Danny will be going with us."

Leilani's grandmother had died a few years back, but her grandfather had arrived a few days ago. And he'd be flying back with them, too. Danny would stay with him, while she and Luke spent time alone. "In fact, our flight leaves at four."

"Well, then let's not keep that handsome doctor waiting." Carrie motioned toward the door.

No, Leilani wouldn't keep Luke waiting. Too much time had passed them by already, and they were both eager to start their life together.

Over the last couple of weeks, Luke had given up the night shift, and Leilani requested a transfer to a womens' shelter in the San Diego area. Everything seemed to be in order. Even Danny was registered at Bayside Elementary, where he would enter sixth grade in the fall.

As she stepped beyond the sliding door and onto the patio, taking care with her white gown, the harpist began to play the wedding march. All heads turned, smiling and nodding, as she began her walk down the grassy aisle, where Luke and Danny awaited her in front of the gazebo.

Luke's gaze never left hers, as she made her way toward her future husband and their son.

He reached out, and she took his hand, as they made the first step in joining their hearts and lives together.

The vows were spoken and tears of joy were shed. Then Luke took Leilani in his arms.

Just before kissing her, he whispered, "I'm going to love you for the rest of my life."

"And I'm going to love you right back."

The kiss was filled with promise, convincing them both that fairy tales really did come true.

* * * * *

Set in darkness beyond the ordinary world.
Passionate tales of life and death.
With characters' lives ruled by laws the everyday
world can't begin to imagine.

n●cture

It's time to discover the Raintree trilogy...

New York Times bestselling author
LINDA HOWARD
brings you the dramatic first book
RAINTREE: INFERNO

The Ansara Wizards are rising and the
Raintree clan must rejoin the battle against
their foes, testing their powers, relationships
and forcing upon them lives they never
could have imagined before...

Turn the page for a sneak preview
of the captivating first book
in the Raintree trilogy,
RAINTREE: INFERNO by LINDA HOWARD
On sale April 2.

Dante Raintree stood with his arms crossed as he watched the woman on the monitor. The image was in black and white to better show details; color distracted the brain. He focused on her hands, watching every move she made, but what struck him most was how uncommonly *still* she was. She didn't fidget or play with her chips, or look around at the other players. She peeked once at her down card, then didn't touch it again, signaling for another hit by tapping a fingernail on the table. Just because she didn't seem to be paying attention to the other players, though, didn't mean she was as unaware as she seemed.

"What's her name?" Dante asked.

"Lorna Clay," replied his chief of security, Al Rayburn.

"At first I thought she was counting, but she doesn't pay enough attention."

"She's paying attention, all right," Dante murmured. "You just don't see her doing it." A card counter had to remember every card played. Supposedly counting cards was impossible with the number of decks used by the casinos, but there were those rare individuals who could calculate the odds even with multiple decks.

"I thought that, too," said Al. "But look at this piece of tape coming up. Someone she knows comes up to her and speaks, she looks around and starts chatting, completely misses the play of the people to her left—and doesn't look around even when the deal comes back to her, just taps that finger. And damn if she didn't win. Again."

Dante watched the tape, rewound it, watched it again. Then he watched it a third time. There had to be something he was missing, because he couldn't pick out a single giveaway.

"If she's cheating," Al said with something like respect, "she's the best I've ever seen."

"What does your gut say?"

Al scratched the side of his jaw, considering. Finally, he said, "If she isn't cheating, she's the luckiest person walking. She wins. Week in, week out, she wins. Never a huge amount, but I ran the numbers and she's into us for about five grand a week. Hell, boss, on her way out of the casino she'll stop by a slot machine, feed a dollar in and walk away with at least fifty. It's never the same machine, either. I've had her watched, I've had her followed, I've even looked for the same faces in the casino every time she's in here, and I can't find a common denominator."

"Is she here now?"

"She came in about half an hour ago. She's playing blackjack, as usual.

"Bring her to my office," Dante said, making a swift decision. "Don't make a scene."

"Got it," said Al, turning on his heel and leaving the security center.

Dante left, too, going up to his office. His face was calm. Normally he would leave it to Al to deal with a cheater, but he was curious. How was she doing it? There were a lot of bad cheaters, a few good ones, and every so often one would come along who was the stuff of which legends were made: the cheater who didn't get caught, even when people were alert and the camera was on him—or, in this case, her.

It was possible to simply be lucky, as most people understood luck. Chance could turn a habitual loser into a big-time winner. Casinos, in fact, thrived on that hope. But luck itself wasn't habitual, and he knew that what passed for luck was often something else: cheating. And there was the other kind of luck, the kind he himself possessed, but it depended not on chance but on who and what he was. He knew it was an innate power and not Dame Fortune's erratic smile. Since power like his was rare, the odds made it likely the woman he'd been watching was merely a very clever cheat.

Her skill could provide her with a very good living, he thought, doing some swift calculations in his head. Five grand a week equaled $260,000 a year, and that was just from his casino. She probably hit them all, careful to keep the numbers relatively low so she stayed under the radar.

He wondered how long she'd been taking him, how long she'd been winning a little here, a little there, before Al noticed.

The curtains were open on the wall-to-wall window in his office, giving the impression, when one first opened the door, of stepping out onto a covered balcony. The glazed window faced west, so he could catch the sunsets. The sun was low now, the sky painted in purple and gold. At his home in the mountains, most of the windows faced east, affording him views of the sunrise. Something in him needed both the greeting and the goodbye of the sun. He'd always been drawn to sunlight, maybe because fire was his element to call, to control.

He checked his internal time: four minutes until sundown. Without checking the sunrise tables every day, he knew exactly when the sun would slide behind the mountains. He didn't own an alarm clock. He didn't need one. He was so acutely attuned to the sun's position that he had only to check within himself to know the time. As for waking at a particular time, he was one of those people who could tell himself to wake at a certain time, and he did. That talent had nothing to do with being Raintree, so he didn't have to hide it; a lot of perfectly ordinary people had the same ability.

He had other talents and abilities, however, that did require careful shielding. The long days of summer instilled in him an almost sexual high, when he could feel contained power buzzing just beneath his skin. He had to be doubly careful not to cause candles to leap into flame just by his presence, or to start wildfires with a glance in the dry-as-tinder brush. He loved Reno; he didn't want to burn it down. He just felt so damn *alive* with all the sunshine pouring down that he wanted to let the energy pour through him instead of holding it inside.

This must be how his brother Gideon felt while pulling lightning, all that hot power searing through his muscles, his veins. They had this in common, the connection with raw power. All the members of the far-flung Raintree clan had some power, some height-ened ability, but only members of the royal family could channel and control the earth's natural energies.

Dante wasn't just of the royal family, he was the Dranir, the leader of the entire clan. "Dranir" was synonymous with king, but the position he held wasn't ceremonial, it was one of sheer power. He was the oldest son of the previous Dranir, but he would have been passed over for the position if he hadn't also inherited the power to hold it.

Behind him came Al's distinctive knock on the door. The outer office was empty, Dante's secretary having gone home hours before. "Come in," he called, not turning from his view of the sunset.

The door opened, and Al said, "Mr. Raintree, this is Lorna Clay."

Dante turned and looked at the woman, all his senses on alert. The first thing he noticed was the vibrant color of her hair, a rich, dark red that encompassed a multitude of shades from copper to burgundy. The warm amber light danced along the iridescent strands, and he felt a hard tug of sheer lust in his gut. Looking at her hair was almost like looking at fire, and he had the same reaction.

The second thing he noticed was that she was spitting mad.

nocturne™

IT'S TIME TO DISCOVER
THE RAINTREE TRILOGY...

There have always been those among us
who are more than human...

Don't miss the dramatic first book by
New York Times bestselling author

LINDA
HOWARD

RAINTREE:
Inferno

On sale May.

Raintree: Haunted by **Linda Winstead Jones**
Available June.

Raintree: Sanctuary by **Beverly Barton**
Available July.

SNLH1BC

//// NASCAR

In February…

Collect all 4 debut novels in
the Harlequin NASCAR series.

SPEED DATING
by *USA TODAY* bestselling author
Nancy Warren

THUNDERSTRUCK
by Roxanne St. Claire

HEARTS UNDER CAUTION
by Gina Wilkins

DANGER ZONE
by Debra Webb

On sale February 2007

And in May don't miss…

Gabby, a gutsy female NASCAR driver,
can't believe her mother is harping at her
again. How many times does she have
to say it? She's not going to help run the
family's corporation. She's not shopping
for a husband of the right pedigree. And
there's no way she's giving up racing!

SPEED BUMPS is one of four
*exciting Harlequin NASCAR books that
will go on sale in May.*

SEE COUPON INSIDE.

www.GetYourHeartRacing.com

NASCARMAY

HARLEQUIN®

Mediterranean NIGHTS™

Tycoon Elias Stamos is launching his newest luxury cruise ship from his home port in Greece. But someone from his past is eager to expose old secrets and to see the Stamos empire crumble.

Mediterranean Nights
launches in June 2007 with...

FROM RUSSIA, WITH LOVE
by *Ingrid Weaver*

Join the guests and crew of *Alexandra's Dream* as they are drawn into a world of glamour, romance and intrigue in this new 12-book series.

www.eHarlequin.com   MN1

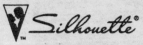 Silhouette®

Romantic
SUSPENSE

Sparked by Danger,
Fueled by Passion.

*This month and every month look for
four new heart-racing romances
set against a backdrop of suspense!*

Available in May 2007

Safety in Numbers
(Wild West Bodyguards miniseries)
by **Carla Cassidy**

Jackson's Woman
by **Maggie Price**

Shadow Warrior
(Night Guardians miniseries)
by **Linda Conrad**

One Cool Lawman
by **Diane Pershing**

Available wherever you buy books!

Visit Silhouette Books at www.eHarlequin.com   SRS0407

REQUEST YOUR FREE BOOKS!
2 FREE NOVELS PLUS 2 FREE GIFTS!

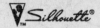

SPECIAL EDITION®
Life, Love and Family!

YES! Please send me 2 FREE Silhouette Special Edition® novels and my 2 FREE gifts. After receiving them, if I don't wish to receive any more books, I can return the shipping statement marked "cancel." If I don't cancel, I will receive 6 brand-new novels every month and be billed just $4.24 per book in the U.S., or $4.99 per book in Canada, plus 25¢ shipping and handling per book and applicable taxes, if any*. That's a savings of at least 15% off the cover price! I understand that accepting the 2 free books and gifts places me under no obligation to buy anything. I can always return a shipment and cancel at any time. Even if I never buy another book from Silhouette, the two free books and gifts are mine to keep forever.   235 SDN EEYU 335 SDN EEY6

Name _____ (PLEASE PRINT)

Address _____ Apt. _____

City _____ State/Prov. _____ Zip/Postal Code _____

Signature (if under 18, a parent or guardian must sign)

Mail to the **Silhouette Reader Service™:**
IN U.S.A.: P.O. Box 1867, Buffalo, NY 14240-1867
IN CANADA: P.O. Box 609, Fort Erie, Ontario L2A 5X3

Not valid to current Silhouette Special Edition subscribers.

Want to try two free books from another line?
Call 1-800-873-8635 or visit www.morefreebooks.com.

* Terms and prices subject to change without notice. NY residents add applicable sales tax. Canadian residents will be charged applicable provincial taxes and GST. This offer is limited to one order per household. All orders subject to approval. Credit or debit balances in a customer's account(s) may be offset by any other outstanding balance owed by or to the customer. Please allow 4 to 6 weeks for delivery.

Your Privacy: Silhouette is committed to protecting your privacy. Our Privacy Policy is available online at www.eHarlequin.com or upon request from the Reader Service. From time to time we make our lists of customers available to reputable firms who may have a product or service of interest to you. If you would prefer we not share your name and address, please check here. ☐

SSE07

They're privileged, pampered, adored...
but there's one thing they don't
yet have—his heart.

THE MISTRESSES

A sensual new miniseries by

KATHERINE GARBERA

Make-Believe Mistress

#1798 Available in May.

His millions has brought him his share of scandal.
But when Adam Bowen discovers an incendiary
document that reveals Grace Stephens's secret
desires, he'll risk everything to claim this very
proper school headmistress for his own.

And don't miss...

In June,
#1802 **Six-Month Mistress**

In July,
#1808 **High-Society Mistress**

Only from Silhouette Desire!

Visit Silhouette Books at www.eHarlequin.com   SDTM0407

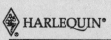

HARLEQUIN®

American ROMANCE®

A THREE-BOOK SERIES BY BELOVED AUTHOR

Judy Christenberry

Dallas Duets

What's behind the doors of
the Yellow Rose Lane apartments?
Love, Texas-style!

THE MARRYING KIND
May 2007

Jonathan Davis was many things—a millionaire,
a player, a catch. But he'd never be a husband.
For him, "marriage" equaled "mistake." Diane Black
was a forever kind of woman, a babies-and-minivan
kind of woman. But John was confident he could
date her and still avoid that trap.
Until he kissed her…

Also watch for:
DADDY NEXT DOOR
January 2007

MOMMY FOR A MINUTE
August 2007

Available wherever Harlequin books are sold.

www.eHarlequin.com   HARM07JC

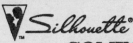

COMING NEXT MONTH

#1825 FROM HERE TO PATERNITY—Christine Rimmer
Bravo Family Ties
Talk about timing—just when Charlene Cooper's high school
sweetheart Brand Bravo breezed back into town, Charlene's little
sister left a baby bundle on her doorstep with a note that Brand was
the father. Now a shocked Charlene had to take Brand to task…and
take on the new wave of attraction she felt for her irresistible first
love.

#1826 ROMANCING THE TEACHER—Marie Ferrarella
After having a car accident while under the influence of medication,
Ian Malone received community service at a homeless shelter, and it
turned out to be a blessing in disguise—because that's where he met
volunteer Lisa Kittridge. Ian was a quick study when it came to this
schoolteacher's charms, but would their mutual secrets prevent the
couple from making the grade?

#1827 ONE MAN'S FAMILY—Brenda Harlen
Logan's Legacy Revisited
When Alicia Juarez turned to P.I. Scott Logan to help get her brother
out of prison, the ex-cop had his doubts about the man's innocence.
But it only took a little while before the pretty nurse with a fierce
commitment to family convinced Logan to take the case…and take a
chance on love.

#1828 HAVING THE COWBOY'S BABY—Stella Bagwell
Men of the West
The last thing Southern belle Anne-Marie Duveuil needed was
to fall for another good-looking, sweet-talking man—the first time
it happened, the heartache almost landed her in a convent! But
when Cordero Sanchez rode into town, the sparks flew, and soon
a special surprise had the die-hard singles rethinking their vow not to
exchange vows….

#1829 MR. RIGHT NEXT DOOR—Teresa Hill
Saved from modern-day pirates during a luxury cruise, Kim Cassidy
returned to Georgia head over heels in love with her rescuer…until
sexy Nick Cavanaugh moved in next door. But would Nick's hidden
agenda—to investigate Kim and catch the crook who had posed as
her "hero"—nip Kim's feelings for her new neighbor right in the bud?

#1830 A MAN TO COUNT ON—Helen R. Myers
On the day of his biggest professional triumph, Judge Dylan Justiss,
a widower, watched as the woman he'd loved from afar, Austin
district attorney E. D. Martel, went down in flames. Risking it all,
Judge Justiss knew it was time to live up to his name and rescue a
wronged woman from a sordid scandal…and rescue his own heart in
the process.

SSECNM0407